TURTLE CLAN
JOURNEY

TURTLE CLAN
JOURNEY

BY LYNDA DURRANT

✵ ✵ ✵

CLARION BOOKS ✵ NEW YORK

1-4062

Clarion Books
a Houghton Mifflin Company imprint
215 Park Avenue South, New York, NY 10003

The text for this book was set in 13-point Caslon.

Printed in the USA

LIBRARY OF CONGRESS CATALOGING-IN-PUBLICATION DATA
Durrant, Lynda, 1956–
Turtle clan journey / Lynda Durrant.
p.   cm.
A sequel to Echohawk.
Summary: As the captive white boy Echohawk and his Mohican father and
brother make a perilous journey from the Hudson River Valley to a settlement
on the Ohio River, Echohawk feels the conflicting pulls of his dual heritage.
ISBN 0-395-90369-6
1. Mohegan Indians–Juvenile fiction. [1. Mohegan Indians–Fiction.
2. Indians of North America–Fiction. 3. Indian captives–Fiction.
4. Identity–Fiction.] I. Title.
PZ7.D93428Tu   1999
[Fic]–dc21   98-22710
CIP
AC
QBP   10 9 8 7 6 5 4 3 2 1

❖ TO WESLEY

※ ※ ※

[Captivity is] an awfull School for Children When We See how Quick they will Fall in with the Indians ways. Nothing Seems to be more takeing. In Six months time they Forsake Father & mother, Forgit thir own Land, Refuess to Speak there own toungue & Seeminly be Holley Swollowed up with the Indians.

—TITUS KING,
RETURNED CAPTIVE OF THE
CANADIAN ABENAKI,
1755–1758

Contents

CHAPTER ONE
STILLWATER

"You can't sleep here, little brother," Echohawk said.

"I will wake up soon," Bamaineo announced as he lay down on a small muddy hill near the river.

A few spikes of icy grass had pushed their way through the frozen mud. As the cold wind lifted the brittle, ice-encrusted grass, it set the blades to rattling. The sound of the quivering grass reminded Echohawk of a turtle-shell rattle full of dried cherry stones.

With a smile on his face Bamaineo stretched out as though the winter-blown hill were a sunny meadow on an endless summer afternoon. There was mud in his hair as he turned his face toward the weak sunshine.

Bamaineo closed his eyes.

"Bamaineo, you cannot sleep here," Echohawk

repeated. He nudged his brother's shoulder with his foot.

The muddy hill sloped to a sodden yard that stretched from the riverbank all the way to a large clapboard house. The house had tall trees surrounding it on three sides to block the wind.

The house was white and had a barn attached to its northern side. The barn was twice as big as the house. A horse and her foal stuck their heads out of a stall window and watched the three travelers. The front windows of the house seemed to watch them too.

"We cannot stop here," Glickihigan said, reaching down to shake his younger son's shoulder. "You will sleep when the sun sleeps, Bamaineo. We have a lot more walking to do before then. Wake up. Do you hear me?"

But Bamaineo was already asleep, or maybe just pretending to be. He'd wrapped his muddy bearskin around his body like a black cocoon. Only the top of his head and his feet poked through.

Glickihigan glanced toward the house. "Echohawk, help me wake your brother. Quickly. If we cannot wake him, I will have to carry him."

Echohawk sat next to Bamaineo and gave the bearskin a hard yank. Sitting down was a mistake. He knew he could not stand up to walk again without some sleep. His muscles and bones seemed to melt into the earth with exhaustion. His body craved sleep—real sleep, for a long time and in a warm, safe place.

For seven suns the royal clan of the Mohicans, the Turtle clan, had been walking south along the west bank of the Muhekunetuk, catching short naps whenever they could hide in barns or behind haystacks. Even then someone always had to stay awake and stand guard.

Echohawk rested his head on his brother's chest. *For a moment, just a moment,* he told himself.

"I, too, will wake up soon," he murmured. At first he was embarrassed. He was thirteen winters—a man!—and he was drifting off to sleep like a little boy. But Bamaineo's beating heart and even breathing were lulling him to sleep quickly.

"Echohawk, you cannot sleep here." His father shook his shoulder. "Wake up. Someone is coming. A man with a musket."

Echohawk forced himself to sit upright. He looked, bleary-eyed, toward the house.

The front door to the house had closed quietly. A man holding a musket was standing on the front porch. The man and his horses watched them closely.

Echohawk sat motionless as the man approached. The man's musket was cocked and ready, the barrel pointed toward Glickihigan's feet.

When the man was close enough to see Bamaineo's feet sticking out of the bearskin, he relaxed his shoulders a little. But the musket still pointed toward Glickihigan.

He was young, perhaps thirty, with a long brown beard and wary eyes as blue as the summer sky.

The only sounds were the rhythmic breathing of Bamaineo's sleep and the gurgling river, swollen with winter runoff to the very edge of the riverbank, as it rushed swiftly past.

"Is there something wrong?" the man asked softly.

Echohawk had spent the winter in school learning English.

"No," he said quickly.

"We are going to Albany," Glickihigan replied in English. "We have been walking for a long time. My sons are tired. If they could sleep here for just a moment."

"You speak English, sir?"

"Yes." Glickihigan pointed to Bamaineo. "I learned your language when I was my son's age."

The man squatted next to Bamaineo, the musket barrel still pointing toward the ground. Echohawk studied it. *A good musket. But not as good as mine.*

"Your sons are sick?"

"No, sir. Just tired. We have been walking for one week, from Saratoga-on-the-Hudson."

The man frowned. "That can't be more than fifteen miles upriver."

"We are carrying so much," Glickihigan replied. "With an eight-year-old, even two miles is a good day."

"And you're tired yourself, sir?" the man asked.

"No, not at all."

The man shook his head as he stood up. "They can't stay here," he said firmly.

"I have told them this, but they're so tired from walking. I can't wake my younger one. Only for a short time, I assure you—"

"You misunderstand me, sir. They'll be sick, sleeping out in the cold. It's not even spring yet. We have an extra bed. If you could lift the little one, sir?"

"A bed?" Echohawk asked. "We can sleep in a bed?"

Glickihigan knelt next to Echohawk. "You see this man's musket?" he whispered in Mohican. "You will walk on one side of him and I will walk on the other."

The man picked up two backpacks and some of the gear, while Glickihigan tossed Bamaineo over his shoulder. Echohawk carried his own backpack and gear toward the house.

Snow still clung to the ground around the trees and in low-lying patches on the lawn. Echohawk's and Glickihigan's moccasins sucked at the wet ground with every step. The man's boots splashed mud to his knees as he walked between them.

A warm, soft wind blew across their faces. It smelled of the sweet earth and sunshine, of wild flowers, ripening berries, and the yearly promise of spring.

Echohawk took a deep sniff, looked at his father, and smiled.

"Smell that southerly wind," the man said agreeably. "In another week I'll be planting."

"Yes," Glickihigan said as he smiled back at his son. "The winter is almost over."

"It could snow again, though," the man said. "That's all right if the seeds haven't sprouted. But if the shoots are up and we have a cold snap. . . ." The man sighed.

"Yes," Glickihigan replied. "At this time of year, anything can happen."

As they stepped into the house, a blond woman and a little blond boy shrank against a far window. The woman held a long iron spoon in her hand. The little boy pressed his head against his mother's skirt. Their faces were as white and rigid as icicles.

To be polite and to show their trust, Echohawk and Glickihigan laid their tomahawks and knives by the front door. They set their muskets against the wall by the doorframe.

Glickihigan laid Bamaineo by the fire, and Echohawk sat next to him. Echohawk's numb feet began to sting as the fire warmed them. His wet moccasins made a hissing sound as they steamed dry. The warm, snug room made him feel sleepy all over again.

"It's all right, Katrina. It's all right, Henry. These boys are tired, that's all," the man said in a soothing voice. He turned to Glickihigan.

"My wife is Dutch and her family had some trouble," the man explained. "They tried to settle along the Mohawk when she was a child." The man sighed again. "She was the only survivor."

"Mohawks?" Echohawk asked.

Katrina tightened her grip on the iron spoon.

"We are not Mohawks. We are Mohicans," Glickihigan said softly. He smiled at her and nodded. "We are going to the west."

"Mohicans?" The man looked surprised. "Katrina, it's all right. Show these boys where they can sleep. It's all right."

Glickihigan switched to Mohican. "Do not wear your clothes while you sleep, Echohawk. They are too muddy. Sleep well. We will leave before dark."

Echohawk rolled Bamaineo out of his bearskin, then hoisted his brother across his shoulders. He followed Katrina and Henry through the house. Along the way they passed paintings on the walls and heavy wooden furniture on floors as smooth and shiny as ice. Dried flowers hung from the ceiling beams, filling the house with their delicate scents.

In the back bedroom logs in a corner fireplace crackled and blazed. Katrina pulled several woolen blankets from a drawer and tucked them around the corners of a huge bed. Henry still clung to her skirts and stared at them, his eyes as big as an owl's.

"Thank you for your kindness," Echohawk said.

Mother and son jumped as though they were one person; both pairs of feet left the floor at the same time. Katrina and Henry ran out of the room backward. They never turned their backs on their guests.

Echohawk stripped Bamaineo down to his skin, pulled the bedclothes back, then flung him onto the bed. The feather mattress almost swallowed him up; Bamaineo just snored loudly.

"I know you are not asleep, little brother. Little brother?"

Echohawk pushed him onto the far side of the bed. He took off his own clothes. Muddy tunics, leggings, moccasins, and breechcloths lay in a pile on the floorboards.

The sheets and pillowcases were made of soft, white cloth. The many blankets were thick and woolen. Echohawk burrowed between the deep feather mattress and the bedclothes. The pillow-cases were scented with pine balsam and flowers. He'd never felt more comfortable in his life.

"I could sleep here forever. Bamaineo? Balsam and flowers and something else," he murmured into his brother's ear. "I smell something else."

"*Cinnamon,*" Bamaineo murmured. "Like Mrs. Warner's apple pies."

While in school, they had spent the winter living with Mr. and Mrs. Warner. Mr. Warner had been their teacher.

"You are awake, little brother."

"No."

"Yes, you are," Echohawk replied. "It is as though we are sleeping next to one of her warm apple pies."

"We are sleeping *in* one of Mrs. Warner's warm apple pies."

Echohawk laughed. "Then Mr. Warner will eat you for his evening corn."

"Only if he can catch me," Bamaineo whispered sleepily.

Black-capped chickadees sang on the bare branches outside the bedroom window. The chickadees, who know how fine and dandy they are, sang, "We are chickadee-dee-dees, we are chickadee-dee-dees," over and over again.

Sleep pulled Echohawk forward—like the strong river current in late winter. His last waking moments were spent listening to the boasting birds and his brother's deep breathing as he slept.

※ ※ ※

"Echohawk." Glickihigan shook his shoulder gently. "Do not wake your brother. Mr. Adam Watkins has something to say to you. It is almost time for evening corn."

Echohawk woke with a start. The chickadees were gone; the sky outside the windows was streaked red and dark blue against the late-afternoon sunset. The last thing he wanted to do was get out of this bed! He hadn't been this warm since the night he and Bamaineo had run away from Mr. and Mrs. Warner's cabin.

Echohawk dressed quickly so he wouldn't get cold again.

"I had almost forgotten what it felt like to be warm and sleepy instead of cold and sleepy," he told Glickihigan.

"The warm spring is coming. Adam Watkins wants to talk to you. I will translate what you do not understand."

"What is wrong, Father?"

Glickihigan wouldn't meet his eyes. "You must think carefully and decide for yourself."

※ ※ ※

"Name's Adam Watkins," the man said back at the fire. Copper kettles, spoons, and cooking pots hung from hooks around the fireplace. A pair of silver candlesticks had pride of place on the mantelpiece. Mr. Watkins' musket hung from the chimney bricks. The fire's reflection flickered and danced on the metal surfaces.

His wife was holding an iron basket over the fire. As she jiggled the long handle, corn began popping inside the basket.

"My name is Jonathan Starr to you, I reckon," Echohawk said hesitantly, looking at his father. When he was at school, all the adults expected him to use his white name.

"Mr. Starr." The man stared hard into Echohawk's face. "You're going to Albany, Mr. Glickihigan?"

"Albany first. I have furs I wish to trade there. Then we will go to the Three Sisters."

"Your three sisters?"

"Yes. Thank you, Mrs. Watkins." Glickihigan accepted a bowl of hot popcorn and a mug of steaming cider from her. Henry still clung to his mother's skirt. When Glickihigan winked at him, Henry began to cry.

"Henry, stop crying at once," Mr. Watkins said crossly. "He's four years old. My wife has been filling his head with Indian stories to make him behave."

Mrs. Watkins gave Echohawk a mug of cider and took Henry to the window seat. She rocked him in her lap until he stopped sobbing.

Glickihigan passed the popcorn bowl to Echohawk. He placed the bowl in his lap and stuffed popcorn in his mouth.

"So you're going to visit your sisters?" the man repeated.

"They're our sisters, but not to your way of thinking," Glickihigan replied. "Where the Allegheny River and the Monongahela River meet the Ohio River. We call them the Three Sisters. You call that place the Fork. We're going to live there."

"Oh, rivers you mean. That's a long way. Over the Catskills, through Iroquois country." He glanced at his wife. "Those Mohawks don't like trespassers."

"We will have to be careful. Still, there are other nations among the Iroquois—the Seneca, the Tuscarora, the Cayuga, the Oneida, and the Onondaga. They're not so fierce, I think."

"You'll leave the Hudson?"

"Yes," Glickihigan said sadly. "We Mohicans call this river the Muhekunetuk. It means 'the water is never still.' But here the water *is* still. I have never seen the Muhekunetuk so quiet."

Mr. Watkins laughed. "I call my farm Stillwater. And Isaac Mann has a mill—perhaps you saw it upriver a bit? Maybe we'll have a town here some-day. By summer the Hudson will be as smooth as glass here in Stillwater. You should see her then."

"Yes, Mr. Watkins, she is a beautiful river," Echohawk said softly. "We will miss her."

A long, uneasy silence grew among them as the three stared at the fire. A pretty blue-and-white china clock on the mantelpiece ticked off the minutes. The farmer cleared his throat a few times before speaking again.

"Mr. Starr, I couldn't help but notice. You're as tall and slender as a Delaware, but you have yellow-brown eyes and brown hair."

"I found him hiding in a log in the forest," Glickihigan said quickly. "He has been with me since he was your Henry's age.

"My son," Glickihigan said to Echohawk in Mohican, "this is what he wants to tell you. Listen carefully." Glickihigan nodded to Adam Watkins.

"You have troubles, sir—troubles I reckon you don't know anything about," said Mr. Watkins. "A few years ago, in October 1743, the Massachusetts General Court offered a Canadian Mohawk and his Massachusetts-born wife, a woman named Eunice Williams, a chance to live in the Bay Colony. She'd been taken as a captive from Deerfield, Massachusetts, as a child. The court offered them a gift of twelve pounds, ten shillings outright, and a yearly gift of seven pounds, ten shillings after that, if they would just leave Canada and come live in Massachusetts. A working man could labor for half the year and not earn twelve pounds. A lot of money, Mr. Starr. A lot of trouble for you as well."

"My trouble? Why do you say that?"

"New York does not want to appear . . . indifferent to the sufferings of her captives. Following Massachusetts' example, our governor, with the help of all the patroons, has been quietly offering ransoms. Ten pounds for any captive brought back to the settlements."

Echohawk's head was spinning. "I don't understand—"

"Any captive, Mr. Starr." Mr. Watkins looked into his eyes and repeated slowly, "*Any* captive."

"Me?" Echohawk sprang to his feet.

"You're safe here," he said quickly. "On my honor, Mr. Starr. Neither my wife nor I will turn you in."

"We didn't know this about the ransom, Mr. Watkins," Echohawk said. He stared into the fire, popcorn and cider forgotten. As he glanced at his musket, his heart began to pound.

A log broke in half and fell onto the hearthstones.

"You can't go to *Albany*, my son," Glickihigan said softly in Mohican. "*Patroon* Henrick van Rensselaer's council fire, his *headquarters*, is there. He is one of the men who pays the *ransoms*."

Mr. Watkins said, "Mr. Starr, you could stay here."

"Here?" Glickihigan and Echohawk said together.

"You would be safe here," he said firmly. "On my honor, Mr. Glickihigan."

Mr. Watkins stood up. "You must be very hungry. My wife has made us a good Dutch dinner. Please stay the night. If you must go to Albany, take your leave after breakfast tomorrow. Mr. Starr, you can always return and hide here."

"You are as kind as we are hungry." Glickihigan stood up and finished his cider. "Thank you for your kindness."

"I will wake Bamaineo," Echohawk said softly. He drank his cider in one long gulp.

※　※　※

Mrs. Watkins set a roast goose with potatoes and applesauce on the table. They ate their evening corn on blue-and-white china plates with heavy silver forks, spoons, and knives.

Then Mrs. Watkins fried up round pieces of dough. While they were hot, she sprinkled them with cinnamon and sugar and heaped them onto a platter.

"Doughnuts," Mrs. Watkins announced.

"Doughnuts," Echohawk said, reaching for a handful.

Halfway through the pile, Echohawk and Bamaineo had cinnamon and sugar all over their faces and in their long braids. The adults were laughing. Even Henry was giggling.

When the doughnuts were gone, they drank more hot cider. Mr. Watkins played the violin. Katrina picked up Henry and danced with him.

The roaring fire and the hot cider made the room feel as warm as if it were the Moon of Ripe Berries. Echohawk began to nod; Mrs. Watkins' dress was a whirling mass of color.

The next thing Echohawk knew, it was morning. The entire Turtle clan was in the feather bed.

"We are chickadee-dee-dees, we are chickadee-dee-dees," he heard again and again through the window.

"Chickadees," Glickihigan groaned as he swung his feet to the floor. "They are always so pleased with themselves."

"And so early in the morning, too," Bamaineo added. "Echohawk, ask her if we can eat *doughnuts* again."

"You ask her," Echohawk replied. "Practice your English."

For morning corn they had cold leftover goose, more applesauce, and tiny pancakes dusted with cinnamon and sugar.

Mrs. Watkins piled more of the tiny pancakes onto the platter. *"Poffertjes,"* she said.

The Turtle clan ate and ate. Echohawk looked longingly at the crackling fire.

I could just stay here, he thought, *put my feet up to the fire, and wait for Glickihigan to return. But what if something happened and my father and brother never returned?*

"Time to go," Glickihigan said.

Echohawk nodded and stood up.

They put on the backpacks and tucked their tomahawks and knives into their belts. Their muskets were still leaning against the doorframe.

Echohawk hadn't noticed the row of wooden shoes by the door. As he examined them, Henry shuffled into the smallest pair. With a big grin on his face Henry clomped, clomped, clomped up and down the planked oak hallway.

Mrs. Watkins laughed and pointed to Henry's shoes. *"Klompen,"* she said.

"Thank you for your food and a place to sleep," Glickihigan said at the front door. "Will you take this beaver pelt for payment? I trapped him on the Ohio River last winter. There are no beavers left on the Muhekunetuk."

Mr. Watkins shook his head. "You don't owe us a thing, sir. Have a safe journey. Be careful through Iroquois country."

"Perhaps I will come back," Echohawk said.

"It would be my honor, Mr. Starr."

"Thank you, Mr. and Mrs. Watkins."

"Thank you, Mr. and Mrs. Watkins." Bamaineo finally spoke up. "Good morning! Good-bye!"

As the Turtle clan walked toward the river, the horse and her foal stuck their heads through their stall window and nickered to them companionably. A flock of geese flapped straight up, then sideways out of the yard, like a white sheet cracking in a stiff wind. When Echohawk and Bamaineo turned to look at the geese, Henry, still wearing his *klompen*, waved at them. They waved back.

The Turtle clan headed for the trees, Echohawk bringing up the rear. He decided to take one more look at the house that might be his hiding place.

"I will catch up," he called out to Glickihigan. He ran up the river path toward the house.

"Adam," Mrs. Watkins was saying. There was something in the tone of her voice that made Echohawk hide behind a tree and listen.

"Adam, why you don't want to collect the ransom on that boy? Why you don't want the beaver pelt? That old Indian was right, he was. There's been no beaver on the Hudson since my grandfather's day."

"Katrina, you know what Indians are like. Family is everything. And those are Mohicans. All this land and the Hudson, too, used to be theirs. They don't owe us a thing."

CHAPTER TWO

RED FOX

Slowly the bare trees filled up with birds. The winter forests, silent and empty for so long, rang with birdsong once again.

As the warm wind blew in from the south, it carried the sweet smell of thawing earth and the birds with it. The branches lit up with color. Purple warblers, golden finches, bluebirds, scarlet tanagers, orange orioles, and others winged their way to their summer homes along the river.

The birds sat in the trees and sang greetings to one another, or flitted about looking for nesting grass and mates. They were much too busy to pay attention to the three weary travelers walking so quietly below them.

Gradually the trees and birdsong thinned out as

Glickihigan, Echohawk, and Bamaineo walked closer and closer to Albany. The trail was no longer a skinny deer path. It had widened to a muddy road filled with traffic. Every time someone passed, Echohawk pulled his wolfskin cap lower over his eyes and turned his face away.

"Now I know how the deer feel, hunted all the time," he muttered to Bamaineo.

"On your right," horseback riders shouted as they trotted past. "On your right, please."

"Give way the road! Give way," a coach driver shouted as a grand coach with four horses trotted past. The passengers didn't even look at them.

"On your right," more horseback riders shouted. The horses trotted through puddles and splashed them with muddy water.

They stopped in a little town for noon corn. The town common was a long, narrow pasture with houses crowded around the edges. But at this time of year the common was mostly mud. Cows munched on hay bundles the townspeople had left along the edges of the pasture.

The Turtle clan found a dry place next to a grove of trees. As the cows moved in for a better look, Glickihigan shouted at them and waved his arms. Echohawk and Bamaineo scooped up snow and threw the last snowballs of winter at the cows. They bellowed and lumbered away.

"I have never seen these trees before, Father," Echohawk said.

"Yes, these trees are from across the Gishik-shawkipet, the Sun's Salt Sea. In late summer, at the Moon of Ripe Berries, these trees give up their fruit. The fruit is called a *peach*. These are *peach* trees. The blossom is very pretty—a delicate pink—and smells as sweet as any locust blossom."

"How did the trees get here?" Bamaineo asked.

"People brought the trees with them when they crossed the Sun's Salt Sea. In my own time I have seen many good things brought to our valley. I have seen *bees, honey, apples, cinnamon, horses, peaches, butter, cloth*."

"*Doughnuts,*" Bamaineo said.

"Yes." Glickihigan laughed. "How could I forget the *doughnuts?* Most of the things are good, some bad."

"The bears like the *honey* the *bees* make," Bamaineo said through a mouthful of dried venison.

"So do you," Echohawk said, poking his brother in the stomach.

"I love *honey,*" Bamaineo replied. "I love *honey* almost as much as maple syrup."

While they rested, they watched a pair of cedar waxwings on a hawthorn bush. The birds were eating the berries left over from summer. They passed a purple berry between them, beak to beak, back and forth, back and forth, until one of them finally ate it.

"He will eat the berry next time, Echohawk," Bamaineo said.

"No, she will, little brother."

The male waxwing ate the berry.

"I was right!" Bamaineo shouted.

"Shh—you will frighten them away," Echohawk said softly.

Back and forth, back and forth, from beak to beak, the cedar waxwings passed the berries between them.

"Do you see, little brother? She is eating almost twice as many berries as he is. Cedar waxwings are so polite, they never want to be the first one to eat. But it is spring, and she needs the extra food for her eggs."

Echohawk said bitterly, "Mr. Watkins said I could hide with his family. But a Mohican warrior does not hide like a rabbit in a rabbit hole."

"Let's go home," Bamaineo said, "to our camp by the waterfall."

"There is no home, no camp by the waterfall, little brother. Don't you remember?" Echohawk asked gently. "A sickness came. Everyone is gone."

They sat in silence, a cold wind blowing. Echohawk thought about the Bear clan and the Wolf clan, faces he knew as well as his own. Faces he would never see again.

Echohawk sighed. "I trust Mr. Watkins but not his wife. When I heard her talking about the *ransom*, I could almost see the ten gold pieces in her eyes. I won't hide . . . but I will wait in the woods for your return."

Glickihigan said, "No. Too much could happen, waiting in the woods alone. There is a Munsee camp not far from here. You can stay with them.

We should start walking again if we are to reach this camp before sundown."

There was a raft waiting for paying passengers just above where the Muhekunetuk met the Mohawk River. Glickihigan traded a fat beaver tail to the raftsman, and the Turtle clan climbed aboard. Echohawk hunched his shoulders and pretended that his feet were the most fascinating things he'd ever seen.

They reached the Munsee camp just before dusk. Glickihigan beckoned Echohawk and Bamaineo to hide behind a fallen log. For a moment they watched and waited.

The camp stretched along the riverbank. There were many wigwams. In the center, fire pits steamed with the smell of cooking food. From behind their log Echohawk saw one wigwam close by. It was standing apart from the others, its smoke drifting alone through the darkening air. There were trees and stacked wood around it, as if the clan that lived there wanted to hide.

Farther downstream was a large building made of logs. It was the largest structure in the camp. As Echohawk studied the building, a wad of snow fell out of a pine tree just above it. Instead of landing on the roof, the snow fell through the building and onto the floor.

That's odd.

Echohawk studied the building. Part of its roof was burned away. Another clump of snow tumbled from the same tree and fell toward the front of the building. The snow hit the roof with a wet splat this time.

Part of the roof is burned. I wonder what happened.

Echohawk's sharp ears picked up a noise just behind him. He kept his body still and turned his head slowly in the direction of the noise.

A young man about Echohawk's age, dressed in moccasins, leggings, breechcloth, and tunic, stood behind them. But he looked like no boy Echohawk had ever seen before. His chest was as wide as a tree trunk and his sturdy arms and legs were as thick as a tree's first branches. Echohawk had a few freckles across his nose, but this one had freckles all over his face and neck, his arms and hands, as many freckles as there were stars in the night sky.

His eyes were the same dark blue as the eastern sky just after sunset. But it was the young man's hair that took Echohawk's breath away. His fiery red hair tumbled in wild curls, waves, and ringlets from his wide forehead all the way down to his waist.

A red-and-black foxtail hung from a silver chain around his thick neck.

As the Turtle clan stood up slowly, the young man brandished his tomahawk. They raised their hands to show they were without weapons.

"Hello," Echohawk said in his own language.

The young man stared at Echohawk in surprise.

"Hello," he replied. "Delaware?"

"Yes. Mohican," Echohawk replied. "Munsee?"

The young man nodded eagerly. "Munsee."

He glanced at Glickihigan and Bamaineo but turned his attention back to Echohawk.

"What is your name?" Echohawk asked. He spoke slowly, for Mohican and Munsee were not quite the same.

The young man smiled for the first time. "As a baby my name was Copper. I came into my name as Red Fox." He had a soft voice for someone so big. "Your name?" he asked.

"Echohawk. My father is Glickihigan; my brother is Bamaineo."

"Your eyes are the same yellow-brown as a hawk's. You were named because of the way you look too." Red Fox gave a satisfied nod. He slipped his tomahawk back into his belt.

"Why are you in the forest all by yourself?" Bamaineo asked.

"There is a *church* here now and two white families. Because of the *ransom,* I have to hide in the forest until the sun goes down so the *missionaries* won't see me. Only then can I go home." He gestured toward the lone wigwam surrounded by trees.

Echohawk nodded. It would be impossible to hide that red hair among the Munsee.

"Why are you here?" Red Fox asked pleasantly.

"We are going to the Three Sisters," Glickihigan answered. "We want to stay near here and rest for a few suns. We have heard about the *ransom.* We will have to be careful."

"I have been hiding for many moons. I know how to be careful." Red Fox smiled at Echohawk. "Stay with my mother, Redbird, and my father, Clever As Two Foxes. The Fox clan. Come."

Red Fox led them to the lone wigwam.

Inside were his parents and his two little sisters. His mother's pinched, worried face lit up as Red Fox drew rabbits out of his waist pouch for her. His little sisters pulled at his thick, freckled hands and squealed until Red Fox sat down.

After introductions were made, they all sat around the starfire—five logs shaped as a star and burning in the center. A hole in the center of the wigwam roof let the smoke out. Redbird gave each traveler a wooden bowl of hot venison broth. The broth had a deep smoky taste. It warmed Echohawk to the root.

For evening corn they had nokekik—parched ground corn—and strips of dried venison.

"I apologize for the food," Redbird said softly. "Our stored food is almost gone. In late spring, by the Fish Running Moon, we will have fresh fish and fresh food again."

"Everything tastes good to hungry travelers." Glickihigan nodded to her. "We are grateful for your kindness."

After evening corn Clever As Two Foxes asked the Turtle clan questions about their camp far to the north by the waterfall. The two little sisters combed Red Fox's hair. They took turns holding a mirror up to him. They shrieked and giggled when Red Fox made funny faces in the mirror.

Soon the little sisters were arguing over whose turn it was to hold the mirror. "It's late," Redbird said firmly. "You two are tired. Go to sleep now."

"It's late, Bamaineo," Glickihigan said from across the starfire. "I will see you in the morning."

Bamaineo and the little sisters fell asleep on the same sleeping platform, huddled together like bear cubs sleeping in the same den.

Glickihigan, Redbird, and Clever As Two Foxes talked together softly around the starfire. Red Fox beckoned Echohawk to sit next to him.

"Echohawk, do you know your story? How you came to live among the Mohicans?" he asked softly.

"Yes. My father and men from our camp killed my white family. I was hiding in a hollow log when it happened. He found me and brought me to my mother's wigwam. Their son had died, so my mother was happy to see me. I was three, maybe four winters. My baby name was Bear Cub because sometimes a mother bear hides her cubs in a hollow log."

"My mother's baby son had died and she tried to kill herself, she was so sad," Red Fox said. "My father knew of a white family with many children. They lived far away from here, and they all had hair the color of a fox's back. Their mother would take the baby boy into the fields with her, but she always left him at the edge of the field near the forest. My father waited until I was asleep in the blankets and her back was turned. He brought me here to my mother as a present. And she was happy again. I was not even walking yet."

"Then you have no memory, Red Fox? About your first life, I mean?"

"No." Red Fox paused. "But you do."

"Yes," Echohawk replied. "But only pieces, like remembering a dream from long ago."

"I think about my first life sometimes," Red Fox said. "I wonder how my life would be, how different it would be. I look at my parents and my sisters and I wonder what I would think about them."

"Sometimes," Echohawk said, "I think about how different I would be if I lived in a *cabin,* and wore *boots* and *cloth* instead of moccasins and deerskins. What must it be like, to think as they think and believe as they believe? I remember my white name. It is Jonathan Starr. Sometimes I look at the English and wonder if any of them knew Jonathan Starr."

"I think about what it would be like to live with people who look like me, who have the same hair and eyes," Red Fox said softly. "It would be pleasing to look into their faces and see my face in theirs. Like a *mirror.*"

"Yes, it would be pleasing," Echohawk replied. "I have often thought that way. But I have also thought that the part of me that really is me would be the same, somehow. Every oak tree looks different—the branches curve in a hundred different ways. But the oak trees' trunks all look the same. We are like the trunks. Does that make sense?"

Red Fox shrugged his shoulders. "There is no *ransom* at the Three Sisters, Echohawk?"

"If there is a *ransom*, we will have to go farther west."

"Is that why you are going to the Three Sisters?"

"My father is a trapper, and he spent the winter at the Three Sisters while my brother and I were in *school*. By the time Glickihigan returned, all the clans in the camp by the waterfall were dead. A white man's sickness came. We have nowhere else to go but to the west."

"Perhaps it is better to leave," Red Fox said softly. "At first hiding was fun. I made friends with the raccoons and watched the fawns grow up. I did no work because I was never here. But I am weary of hiding all the time. The winters are cold without a fire.

"It has become more dangerous because the *church* roof burned at the Moon of Deep Snow. Many of the *pews* burned, and the *Bibles*. The *ransom* would pay for a new roof, and *Bibles*, and *pews*."

"The Munsee would not turn you in," Echohawk exclaimed. "Your own people!"

"My father says they would not, but some of them look at me and I see in their eyes new *Bibles*, *pews*, and a roof."

Red Fox tossed a handful of pine needles into the starfire. The pine needles caught fire, glowed red for an instant, then collapsed. "Delaware rest here all the time before leaving for the Three Sisters. We see

Munsees from the far north, Mohicans from other camps, even Raritans and Minisinks from the south. But our camp has always been here. We would never leave."

"The Three Sisters is a good place," Echohawk replied eagerly. "The rivers are deep and swift. There are plenty of fish and deer along the banks. We Delaware will be left alone. My father, brother, and I are Turtle clan. Perhaps someday I will be a sachem—"

"It is late," Glickihigan called from across the starfire.

"Remember, Red Fox," Clever As Two Foxes said, "it is almost spring and warmer now, so the sun throws off his night blanket earlier and earlier. Before the dawntime will come soon enough."

"Good night," Echohawk and Red Fox said together.

Echohawk stretched out close to the starfire. Despite the layer of pine needles on the ground, the wigwam floor was hard and cold. He thought about the soft feather bed in the Watkins' house and the warm blankets. How strange, he thought, to raise geese as though they were children, eat them, then use their feathers for beds and pillows. He remembered the pretty blue-and-white plates, the *applesauce* and *doughnuts*. He thought about Mr. Watkins' music while his wife and son danced. There were windows to fill the home with light and to keep the winter wind outside.

The hanging flowers made the whole house smell like spring.

"So many comforts," he whispered to himself. "Such an easy, soft life."

But Redbird's wigwam smelled like home! Every scent was familiar—the wood smoke of the starfire, the clean smell of the birchbark walls, the smoky-sweet smell of the furs they used for bedding. As he turned over and away from the starfire, he crushed the pine needles beneath him. They too gave off their spicy scent.

Echohawk smiled. Redbird's wigwam had pine needles piled up where the floor met the wigwam walls. How many times had he watched his own mother take a turkey wing and brush the pine needles away from her walls? Somehow the needles always ended up against the walls again.

Red Fox is right, he thought. *It is dangerous to stay here. Although it smells like home, we can't stay here for very long.*

"Echohawk," Red Fox whispered next to him, "I have to hide before the dawntime. I will see you at sundown tomorrow."

"No. Wake me. I want to hide with you."

Chapter Three
HIDING

"Echohawk."

He opened his eyes and saw Red Fox crouching above him, shaking his shoulder.

"Echohawk, wake up."

"I am awake, Red Fox," Echohawk said. He stretched and rolled toward the fire.

It was dark inside the wigwam. The Fox clan's starfire cast flickering shadows against the birchbark walls. The other sleeping faces were lit with orange firelight.

Redbird was awake too. She was stoking the starfire and packing food into a leather bag. Her movements were quick and quiet. *Just like a bird's,* Echohawk thought.

"We let you sleep. I have been awake much longer than you have," Red Fox said with a smile.

"I said I was awake," Echohawk said crossly.

Redbird spooned hot cornmeal sweetened with maple syrup into two bowls. Echohawk and Red Fox ate their morning corn hurriedly and without talking.

They shrugged into their backpacks and slung quivers full of arrows across their right shoulders, and bows across their left shoulders. Redbird walked outside with them. It was cold, and the false dawn was as gray as a gun barrel. There was no wind; the trees were still. Not even the birds were awake.

Near the church the cabins where the white families lay sleeping were dark and quiet.

"No one in the *cabins* is awake, but you must leave now," Redbird said anxiously. She reached up and cupped Red Fox's face in her hands. "Red Fox, every time you hide, I am afraid I will never see you again," she whispered. Her eyes filled with tears.

Red Fox ducked his head in embarrassment. "I have been hiding for a long time. I know how to hide," he said gruffly.

"Mothers know how to worry," Redbird replied. "Be careful, both of you. We will see you at sundown."

❖ ❖ ❖

They were well away from camp when the last of

32

the stars faded away. At sunrise the eastern sky turned pale yellow, then white, then blue. The birds twittered themselves awake and began to swoop and dive to the forest floor, looking for worms and seeds for their morning corn.

Red Fox had been right the night before. It was fun hiding in the woods all day.

They spent the morning hunting in the trees. Red Fox's hunting technique reminded Echohawk of a long time ago, before his mother died, before he went to school to learn English. Just as they were doing now, Echohawk used to sit in a tree, absolutely motionless, and shoot small game with his bow and arrows as the animals foraged below him.

As they walked from hunting ground to hunting ground, Echohawk was impressed that someone as bulky as Red Fox could be so light on his feet. The two of them made no more noise than a breeze rustling through the forest.

They were careful to walk in stops and spurts: Not like people walking with someplace important to go, but like animals foraging in the bushes for food. They stopped—and rustled a few branches. And went on. And stopped—and rustled a few branches. Echohawk and Red Fox sounded just like hungry bears or deer as they made their way farther and farther northwest from the Munsee camp.

When they had each shot three rabbits, Echohawk felt hungry.

"Red Fox, it must be time for noon corn,"

Echohawk said. "My stomach is growling like a bear."

It was early spring, the Earth Drying Moon, but there were no leaves on the trees yet. Shielding their eyes, Red Fox and Echohawk gazed up at the sky, something they could rarely do in deep woods in the summer, when the leaves are full and the forest is in almost permanent shade. The sun shone directly above them.

"Time for noon corn," Red Fox agreed. "Come. I want to show you something."

They headed northwest, following the Mohawk River but walking well away from its banks. Red Fox led Echohawk up a steep deer path and onto level ground. At the edge of the level ground was a small log cabin with rough fields behind it. A breeze pulled a curl of smoke out of the chimney.

Echohawk gasped. "They will see us!"

Red Fox laughed. "They are an old farmer and his wife. I have walked right by them when they are in the fields. They neither see me nor hear me. They must be deaf and blind."

They darted behind trees until they were well away from the cabin and the old farmer's fields. Red Fox led Echohawk down a ravine. The ravine opened up to a marsh.

On an island in the marsh were four tamarack trees growing close together. Their branches swept the ground. Red Fox ducked among the tamarack branches, and Echohawk followed.

Hidden by the branches was a tiny wigwam, no

bigger than a medicine hut. There was just enough room inside for two people.

When his eyes adjusted to the dimness, Echohawk saw skins on the floor and a few crossed and burned sticks in the center of the wigwam. There was a small hole in the center of the roof to let out the smoke.

"You have fires in here," he exclaimed. "Someday you will be found, Red Fox! Even a deaf and blind old farmer can follow a smoke trail with his nose."

Red Fox stuck his jaw out. "I have been hiding for a long time. I know more about hiding than you ever will. During the summer moons I get hungry. I come here to cook some evening corn for myself before I go home. I don't keep the fire burning."

Echohawk shook his head.

"Then I will show you how safe we are," Red Fox stubbornly. "Unless you are too much of a coward to see."

Red Fox left in a huff. When he came back, he was holding brown pine needles in his fists and kindling in his thick, freckled arms. Red Fox lit a fire by striking two flints together. He skinned and gutted one of the rabbits Echohawk had shot and spitted the rabbit over the crackling fire.

Echohawk watched uneasily as smoke poured out of the smoke hole in the roof. The roasting rabbit smelled delicious, but couldn't anyone else smell this rabbit cooking over the fire?

When it was cooked, Red Fox cut the steaming

rabbit lengthwise and flung the halves onto chunks of wood to cool. The food bag Redbird had packed for them was full of parched corn. Red Fox found a small leather pouch at the bottom of the pack. In the pouch was a cache of dried sweet cherries soaked in corn oil.

Red Fox smiled when he saw the cherries. "My mother guessed you would like dried sweet cherries as much as I do. She packed these as a treat for us."

They were hungry from hunting all morning. As Echohawk gnawed at his rabbit half and ate his share of the nokekik, he kept listening for human sounds—steady footsteps, voices, the clink of metal against metal.

Pine sap in a piece of kindling popped like gunfire. Echohawk seized Red Fox's knife and sprang to his knees.

Red Fox rolled onto his back and laughed and laughed. "I have been hiding here for thirteen moons, Echohawk," he shouted as he wiped tears from his eyes. "No one has ever found this wigwam. I set crossed twigs at the door flap. I know just what they are supposed to look like, and they have never been disturbed. A good trick, right? I told you, that old farmer is stupid. I have walked within fifty paces of him and he has never seen me."

"Perhaps he is pretending not to see you. Perhaps they both are pretending."

"What do you mean?" Red Fox demanded.

"Perhaps they are afraid and are waiting for the

soldiers to come and capture you. Perhaps they are waiting for their son to come home to catch you, because the old man's son is stronger than he is. Perhaps they think you are a French trapper on Munsee land and are waiting for the Munsee to capture you. Perhaps they think you are a runaway *soldier* and are waiting for the English to capture you. The old man and his wife could have many reasons for doing nothing that you do not know about."

"But my crossed twigs—"

"Maybe they saw the twigs and know the trick. Maybe they recrossed them after looking inside your wigwam so you would not suspect them. If Mr. Adam Watkins, a farmer up north in *Stillwater,* knows about the *ransom,* then this old farmer and his wife must know too."

Red Fox chewed on a rabbit leg and stared at the smoke, thinking. He threw his rabbit bones into the fire.

"This land is no longer Munsee land, and you worry too much," Red Fox said crossly after a while. "The old farmer and his wife are stupid. And blind and deaf.

"The smoke is caught in the tamarack branches," Red Fox explained as he stretched out. He kicked dirt onto the fire then stretched his thick feet out the door flap. "You see, I have thought of everything. After our nap I will show you a creek where we can drink water. We will eat our cherries after our drink."

"Nap? You're going to sleep in the middle of the afternoon?"

Red Fox sighed. "If you had been hiding as long as I have, Echohawk, you would understand. Sleeping uses up the sun time. After our drink at the creek we can start home again."

Echohawk lay down on his side of the wigwam. "I do not understand you, Red Fox. Why take so many chances? I would never walk past an Englishman's home, or light a fire and roast rabbits, or go to sleep so a *ransom* hunter could sneak up on me."

Red Fox sighed again. "At first hiding was like a game. But then it became too easy, too boring. I take chances to make the game more exciting . . . to make my life more exciting. Once, during the Moon of Longest Days, I ran all the way to *Menands* and back. Just to see if I could do it and not get caught."

"Why?"

"Go to sleep, Echohawk. When you are hiding, even sleeping is exciting, taking a chance. You will see."

Echohawk stretched out on his side of the wigwam. Greasy smoke from the tiny cookfire still flowed upward and out of the smoke hole in the roof. He was determined not to sleep, but he was still tired from walking downriver. Soon his eyelids began to droop.

"Echohawk," Red Fox said softly. "You . . . you do not travel with your mother?"

"No," Echohawk whispered.

"I am sorry."

"You are lucky to have Redbird. More than you know."

Red Fox yawned. "She worries too much."

※ ※ ※

By the fourth sun of hiding, Glickihigan and Bamaineo had made themselves at home in the Munsee camp. They took long naps in the afternoon, and Glickihigan traded two badger skins for one hundred strips of dried, smoked venison.

And Echohawk was as bored as Red Fox. They hid behind trees and threw stones at the old farmer's roof, just to see if he would come out. When the old farmer did come out, brandishing his musket, Red Fox yipped like a fox, then howled like a wolf. They laughed as the old man yelped and dashed inside his home for cover. They laughed even harder when the old man's wife ran out, pointing the musket in the air.

They swam in the Muhekunetuk and the Mohawk, shouting and dunking each other in the icy-cold water. They dared each other to see who could stay in longer, and Echohawk usually won.

On the seventh sun Red Fox yipped like a fox as he crawled shivering out of the Mohawk. The part of him that never saw the sun had no freckles. Now that part was bright red.

"Look behind you," Echohawk shouted. "Yours

is as red as a maple leaf in the Sky-Bears Moon."

"At least mine is not as white as a dead fish's belly," Red Fox shouted back.

"Neither is mine."

As Echohawk stepped out of the water to look behind him, Red Fox pushed him in again. But Echohawk was fast. He grabbed Red Fox's arm, and they both tumbled shouting and splashing into the river.

"All men to starboard! Look lively now!"

"Someone is coming," Red Fox whispered.

They ducked behind trees just as a flatboat full of soldiers raced by in the swift current. The soldiers were scrambling to the right side and paddling furiously. In front of them a boulder jutted out of the river.

Echohawk held his breath. The soldiers were close enough for him to see their red coats, their frightened eyes, and their tight, worried mouths.

His clothes and Red Fox's were on the riverbank! A pile of deerskin leggings, shirts, breechcloths, and backpacks lay in plain sight on shore. The foxtail on Red Fox's necklace ruffled in the breeze.

The soldiers paddled hard, but the hull of the flatboat still scraped against the midstream boulder. As the flatboat rushed by, not one soldier glanced at the pile of clothes.

"Blind, deaf, *and* stupid," Red Fox said. He howled like a wolf and laughed when the soldiers paddled even harder to get away.

"Too bad we cannot tell anyone about fooling the *soldiers*. Right, Echohawk?"

"Right," Echohawk said softly, his heart pounding. The flatboat disappeared as it followed the curve of the river.

⁂

Before evening corn that night Glickihigan squeezed one of Echohawk's long braids and frowned as water trickled out. "We leave tomorrow before the dawntime," he said severely. "Swimming in the Mohawk is not hiding."

"You are right, Father," Echohawk said. "We saw *soldiers* on the Mohawk this afternoon."

"Echohawk!" Red Fox shouted.

"Shh," Redbird said. "Someone will hear you."

"What are you thinking?" Clever As Two Foxes shouted at his son. "Echohawk doesn't know any better, but you do! Hiding is not a game."

"Echohawk knows better," Glickihigan said sadly. "That is why we must leave."

"We see the rabbit skins you give to your mother every night. You skin them, then roast them over fires!" Clever As Two Foxes shouted. "She does not pack enough food for you? Do you think we haven't noticed your hair wet from swimming? There are *soldiers* in their canoes as flat as water in a bowl, going up and down the rivers now that the ice is gone. You have a fox's fur, but not his cleverness. You make your mother worry from sunrise to sunset."

"Red Fox, you will be caught. They will send you to *Albany* or *Boston*," his mother said in a soft but frantic voice.

"We will never see you again," one of the little sisters whispered.

"We hid from those *soldiers*," Red Fox boasted. He looked at his father. "I howled like a wolf and they paddled away, as afraid as women. The English are stupid."

"If we are not stupid, then they are not stupid," Clever As Two Foxes said grimly. "You will stay here, in your mother's wigwam, from sunrise to sunset from now on."

"You have said that before," Red Fox muttered.

"Your brother needs the rest, but we must leave tomorrow, Echohawk," Glickihigan said. "We will hide you in the forest, alone, and meet you later when we return from *Albany*."

"Red Fox, you are fourteen winters," Clever As Two Foxes shouted. "There're men your age who are married! Who would marry a man who acts like a boy?"

"Shh—someone will hear you," Redbird whispered. "Shh."

Red Fox sat cross-legged in front of the starfire with his arms folded across his chest. His lips were pressed together as hard and thin as a bowstring.

"I have been meaning to ask you, Red Fox. Why

don't you hunt with the men?" Echohawk asked. "That's like hiding."

"He makes too much noise when he hunts," Clever As Two Foxes replied gruffly. "He scares away the deer."

"But he's so quiet," Echohawk said.

When he wants to be.

"He's a good hunter," Echohawk continued. "We have come back with rabbits at each sunset."

Red Fox looked up, his eyes full of hope. "Just as I told you, Father. I have learned how to be quiet."

They all watched Clever As Two Foxes, waiting to see what he would say.

Finally: "All right, Red Fox. The next time a hunting party leaves camp, you may go with us."

Red Fox caught Echohawk's eye and grinned. Echohawk grinned back and nodded.

"Echohawk," Bamaineo said, pulling on his brother's sleeve, "how many *soldiers* did you see?"

"Even one is too many, little brother."

❖ ❖ ❖

Red Fox was gone by the time the Turtle clan woke the next morning. Redbird packed enough food in their backpacks for two meals each.

"You must leave before the white families wake up and see you," she said, shooing the Turtle clan out into the dawntime. She joined them outside.

"Echohawk." Redbird pushed something into his hand. "My son is too proud and shy to say this himself, but he will miss you. He is lonesome, hiding by himself every day. He will remember you for a long time."

Redbird's present was the same small leather bag, stuffed with dried cherries and blueberries.

"Thank you. I will also remember him, because we have so much in common, Redbird."

"Yes," she said smiling at him. "Yes, you do."

CHAPTER FOUR

THE HAWK

As they headed downstream, Echohawk thought he caught just a whiff of roasting rabbit. He shook his head and smiled. It was much too early for noon corn. And yet someone as big as Red Fox would need many rabbits to keep from going hungry.

Later the Turtle clan found a grove of pine trees with a spring purling out of the ground. They stopped to eat and rest.

"I will miss Red Fox," Echohawk said through a mouthful of nokekik. He pulled his wolfskin cap down around his eyes. "But I don't want to spend my life hiding."

"In the Ohio country you will not have to hide," Glickihigan said. "At first I thought it was good, you making friends with Red Fox. But he takes too many foolish chances and is not strong enough to admit when he is wrong. Foolish chances and testing one's courage are not the same thing."

"Are there *doughnuts* in *Albany?*" Bamaineo asked.

"You will see for yourself," Glickihigan said, smiling. "If so, we will trade for them and bring some back to your brother."

Echohawk sighed.

"We will find a place for you to hide—"

"A warrior does not hide!"

"To stay," their father corrected himself. "I will trade my furs, and we will leave for the Three Sisters as soon as possible."

"Bamaineo, I have something almost as good as *doughnuts*. Look." Echohawk pulled Redbird's present out of his waist pouch. Bamaineo squealed as he opened the bag full of dried fruit.

They drank their fill of cold spring water and chewed on the dried cherries and blueberries last, so the taste would stay in their mouths longer.

"Cherries and blueberries taste so good!" Bamaineo said as he jumped up and down. "Better than *doughnuts!* Better!"

"You are rested, Bamaineo?" Glickihigan asked in a tired voice. He stood up and rubbed his legs.

Echohawk looked closely at his father. Glickihigan was panting softly as he strapped his backpack. A small groan bubbled from his lips.

Bamaineo is not the one who needs the rest.

Echohawk hesitated. "You will trade all your furs in *Albany?*"

"Yes, I hope so."

"Your burden will be lighter then."

Glickihigan stood up taller and gave Echohawk a sharp look.

"The Three Sisters is so far away," Echohawk stammered.

"We will be there by the Moon of Longest Days," his father snapped. "Assuming you can keep up with me."

✦ ✦ ✦

It was midafternoon when a hawk dipped and wheeled in the sky above their heads. His wingspan cast a shadow on the river road, and the sunlight burnished his feathers to a red-gold brilliance.

"Cur-aack! Cur-aaack!" the hawk cried out in the still air.

The hawk pressed his wings close to his body and plunged toward the river. About a hand's width from the water he cut his dive short. He flew upward, then glided to a low-lying branch of a hemlock next to the riverbank. The hemlock branch dipped and swayed with the hawk's weight.

The hawk was less than an arm's length from the Turtle clan. He was so close, Echohawk saw individual feathers and the gleaming black of his sharp talons. The hawk had fierce yellow-brown eyes. He stared hard at Echohawk. The hawk's cold, piercing gaze cut into Echohawk's heart like a winter wind.

"Cur-aack! Cur-aaack!"

Echohawk's feet rooted to the riverbank in terror. He trembled all over as his heart pounded in his chest. Cold fear washed over him like an ice-laden wave.

The hawk ruffled his wings and stared deeper into Echohawk's eyes.

"Spirit-brother, spirit-helper," Echohawk whispered with a mouth as dry as brown pine needles. "Why are you here? Why do I need protecting?"

The hawk turned his face slowly westward, then flashed his eyes back to Echohawk. The hawk's gaze cut into him again. He fluttered his wings and crouched low.

"What are you trying to tell me?"

"Halt!"

A flatboat of soldiers landed just behind them. Men swarmed out of the flatboat, shouting and aiming pistols at the Turtle clan.

The hawk tried to warn me!

In a burst of speed the hawk flew westward, and Echohawk raced after him.

"Echohawk, wait!" Glickihigan shouted.

"As you were!"

The soldiers splashed through the mud after Echohawk.

He tore through a farmyard. Frantic chickens

and geese squawked in his face; the farm dogs nipped at his heels.

A pistol fired, then another.

The trees, the forest, Echohawk thought, panting for breath. *Follow the hawk to safety.*

A hand grazed his shoulder, touched his braids.

Echohawk bounded over the farm fence and kept running. The trees were just ahead.

Still another pistol blasted. He smelled the gunpowder. The hawk flew straight as an arrow into the forest.

Echohawk tripped on a tree root and shot forward like a felled deer. Immediately hands pulled him to his feet.

"You're all right now, lad. Do you speak any English at all? Any English at all, lad?" A man wearing a red coat was shouting at him. The man's forehead and cheeks were crisscrossed with long scars, like a fishing net drawn across his face.

Glickihigan jumped over the farm fence and crashed into his son. They both toppled to the ground.

"It is my fault!" Echohawk screamed. "Red Fox and I made too much noise! It is my fault!"

"No, you must not think that." Glickihigan tried to help his son to his knees, but it was Echohawk helping his father to stand as the old man gasped for breath. "It was not your fault."

"We can run," Echohawk screamed.

"Listen, listen to me. My son, listen," Glickihigan panted hoarsely into Echohawk's ear.

"We must speak softly—I don't know how much of our language they understand."

"We can run!" Echohawk screamed again.

"They will take you to *Albany*—"

"No!"

"Listen," Glickihigan said. He gasped for breath and tried to whisper at the same time. "They will take you to *Albany* to find your white family. But you do not have white family in *Albany*."

"We can run to the west!" Echohawk shouted. "We can run faster than these men! My spirit-brother will show us—"

"LISTEN!" Glickihigan shook Echohawk's shoulders hard. "I have thought about this moment ever since I found you. Thought about what to do."

Glickihigan cupped his hands around Echohawk's face. The man with the face like a fishing net stood right behind them. The soldiers stood in a circle around them, their pistols pointed and ready.

Glickihigan took another deep breath. He reminded Echohawk of a fish out of water, gasping hopelessly for air.

"Listen very carefully," he said softly. "My son, they will take you to another family. You must pretend to be happy with this other family."

"How can I do that?"

"You must! Listen!" Glickihigan whispered fiercely. "If you pretend to be happy, this family will let their guard down. They will stop watching you. When they stop watching you, your brother and I will be waiting. Do you understand what I am saying, Echohawk?"

"Yes. Yes, I understand," Echohawk whispered eagerly. "But where? Where can I find you?"

"We will find you," Glickihigan whispered in his son's ear. "We will never leave the Muhekunetuk without you. Never. You will start pretending now. Give me your weapons—they will take them from you anyway. You will see them and us again. Soon."

Bamaineo came up to them. He stuffed his hands into his mouth and stared.

"He will give you no trouble," Glickihigan said to the men in English. "We have said our farewells. He is ready to go with you."

"Bamaineo," Echohawk said sadly, squeezing his brother's shoulder. "Good-bye, Bamaineo."

Echohawk gave Glickihigan his tomahawk, his knife, and the musket he'd named Thunderpath.

"I want Bamaineo to have Thunderpath."

"You will need Thunderpath, Echohawk," Glickihigan replied. "There are many deer at the Three Sisters. You will see these deer yourself when we are living there."

"The company will surround the prisoner," the man with the crisscrossed face shouted.

"Glickihigan," Echohawk whispered. "Father—"

The soldiers made a circle around Echohawk and marched him to the flatboat. Glickihigan and Bamaineo followed silently.

"Your money, sir." The man with the crisscrossed

face dropped a cloth bag into Glickihigan's hand.

"My . . . my what?" Glickihigan stammered.

"Your ransom—for a captive, sir."

When the coins jingled together in his palm, Glickihigan jerked his hand away as though the bag were filled with snakes. The bag fell to the ground. Coins spilled out into the mud.

"He's my son."

The man shrugged his shoulders and scooped up the coins.

Echohawk stepped aboard the flatboat and walked to the stern. Glickihigan and Bamaineo stood on the riverbank as the soldiers used oars to push the flatboat into midstream. Bamaineo was crying.

Echohawk's father and brother became smaller and smaller as the flatboat gathered speed. The hawk dipped and wheeled in the sky overhead.

"Cur-aack! Cur-aaack!"

The hawk's cries, and his brother's, became fainter and fainter as the flatboat slipped away.

"Do you have a name, lad?" a soldier asked him. "An English name?"

"Jonathan. Jonathan Starr," Echohawk whispered.

"Starr?" an officer asked in surprise. He peered into Echohawk's face. "Aye. You're a Starr, all right.

"Major," he shouted to the man with the crisscrossed face.

"What is it?" The three men stood over him.

"Major Woodbridge, this boy says he's a Starr. He says his name is Jonathan Starr."

"Starr, is it? Aye, he looks like one with those eyes. Won't she be surprised? Bring him to the bow of the boat, Captain."

"Yes, sir."

"She?" Echohawk asked. "Who is she?"

"You speak English, too," Major Woodbridge said. "You haven't been a captive for long, then. Good. This way, lad."

At the bow were five other captives. Two men in chains sat whispering together. Two little blond girls who looked like sisters were huddled in the corner whimpering. They looked to be eight or nine winters.

By himself, chained and sobbing like a wounded bear, was Red Fox.

CHAPTER FIVE

ALBANY

"Red Fox! You were so sure you wouldn't get caught, and now in your anger you have betrayed me!"

Echohawk lunged at him. As they fell over, Echohawk started punching Red Fox's chest and face.

"How could I tell them?" Red Fox shouted back.

Soldiers gripped Echohawk's arms. They picked him up and threw him across the deck to the other side of the boat. He landed with a bone-jarring thud against the hull.

"Troublemaker, are you?" The man with the crisscrossed face stepped on Echohawk's wrist.

Echohawk gritted his teeth to keep from crying out.

"Watch them both," the man ordered one of the soldiers as he took his foot off Echohawk's wrist.

"Yes, sir."

As Echohawk crawled toward the other captives, Red Fox turned his head away and wiped the tears from his face with the back of his sleeve. Echohawk sat down next to him.

"How could you betray me?" Echohawk whispered through clenched teeth. "How could you tell them I was walking downriver?"

"Yes, exactly. How could I betray you, when I do not speak a word of their language?" Red Fox replied.

"Oh. I—I didn't think of that," Echohawk stammered. "I'm sorry, Red Fox."

"Echohawk, in bright sunlight your hair is reddish brown. No one in the Turtle clan notices anymore. I saw these *soldiers* pointing at your hair."

"I was so careful to hide my face; how could I forget my hair?" Echohawk said in a hollow voice. "How did the *soldiers* find you, Red Fox?"

"The old farmer and his wife showed them my wigwam. I was sleeping inside when they captured me."

"Did they take you back to the Munsee camp? So you could say good-bye to your parents and sisters?"

"No," Red Fox whispered. "They think I am still hiding. The Fox clan won't know anything is wrong until I don't return home."

"My spirit-helper and spirit-brother, the hawk, tried to warn me, but I was too slow in understanding him."

"Echohawk, you made too much noise when you threw the stones on the *cabin* roof. It was you who gave me away."

"Me!" Echohawk shouted. The soldier guarding them poked Echohawk's leg with his boot.

"You threw more stones than I did," Echohawk whispered harshly. "You were laughing so hard when the farmer ran inside and his wife came out instead, your face was as red as your hair. You roasted rabbits and built your wigwam too close to the old farmer's home. He smelled your smoke and saw your feet sticking out of the wigwam as you slept. You told me you like to take chances."

Red Fox jutted his jaw out as far as he could. "Then they smelled the fear on you, when we were roasting rabbits. It was your fear that gave me away. And you were laughing too."

"I am not the reason they caught you."

"It was your fault!"

"Have you ever noticed, Red Fox? Nothing is ever your fault."

Red Fox scowled and studied his bound feet for a moment. "What will they do to us, Echohawk?"

"My father said they will give us to *Albany* families. Or they will try to find your clan from your first life, Red Fox. The one with all the children with hair like a fox's back."

"You must think of a way for us to escape, because it is your fault I was caught, Echohawk."

A hot reply was on Echohawk's lips when one of the bound men called out to them. "Little brothers, where are you from?"

"The Munsee camp by the Mohawk River," Red Fox called back.

"I lived far to the north, in a Mohican camp by the great waterfall," Echohawk added. "But I have not been there since the last Green Corn Moon. I was in *school*, in *Saratoga-on-the-Hudson*, with my brother."

The last three words came out in a whisper. Echohawk looked away, his eyes filled with tears.

"Little brothers, listen to me," the man said. The chains on his wrists and ankles clinked and clanked as he crawled toward them. "We are planning an escape," he said in a low voice. "When it is dark, we will kill as many *soldiers* as we can, then jump over the side. Join us. You will see your clans again."

Sitting behind the first man, the second man shook his head as a warning.

"My father said they will give me to an *Albany* clan," Echohawk replied. "He told me that if I pretend to be happy living with them, they will stop watching me. Then I can escape."

"They will never stop watching you," the man whispered fiercely. His gray eyes smoldered with rage. "Escape now. And kill as many as you can while escaping."

"But you will sink, Uncle, with the chains on your wrists and ankles," Echohawk said. "And you have no weapons."

"We will escape," the man said stubbornly.

"I will take my father's advice. But thank you for trying to help me."

"Thank you for trying to help," Red Fox said. "But since he is the reason I was captured, my friend is already thinking of a way we can escape on our own."

"It was not my fault, Red Fox!" Echohawk shouted.

The man scuttled away and sat scowling against the hull of the flatboat. The second man crawled toward them.

"Do not listen to Smoke Eyes," the second man said softly. "This is the fourth time he has been caught. He has a wife and many children, far to the north near the Canadas. I know more of their language than he does; I have heard the *soldiers* talking. They are sending Smoke Eyes across the Sun's Salt Sea to his clan in *Ireland* this time. He does not know this yet."

"What are we to do?" Red Fox asked.

"Echohawk, what is your father's name?"

"Glickihigan."

"I know of him. He is a wise man. You will take his advice, little brothers. Pretend to be happy. Relieved. They will stop watching you, and you can escape then."

"And the little sisters, Uncle?" Red Fox nodded to the little girls. They were curled up in the bow of the boat, whimpering in their sleep. The soldiers had made a mattress for them out of their bearskin knapsacks.

The second man shook his head. "They are too young to take with us. Their parents will grieve for them."

"What is your name, Uncle?" Echohawk asked.

The man grinned. He rolled up his sleeves to

reveal arms even more freckled than Red Fox's. "My name is Fawn. I am as speckled as a fawn."

"Fawn, will you escape with Smoke Eyes?" Red Fox asked.

"No. But I will wait for a good moment to escape. And I will pretend to be happy, like you. My wife has just had a baby girl. She will wait for me to return; then we will go west. Tell me, little brothers, how much of their language do you understand?"

"None," Red Fox answered. "I have no memory of my first life."

"Some," Echohawk replied. "I can understand more than I can speak."

"You must pretend to understand no English, Echohawk. They will talk about you right in front of your face. You will learn a lot if you pretend to understand nothing."

"I told them my English name. I asked them a question."

"It is best to tell them nothing," Fawn answered.

A soldier cuffed Echohawk's hands and feet together. Now they were all bound except for the little girls. Extra guards stood around Smoke Eyes.

※　※　※

Later the savory smell of meat, carrots, and onions steamed out of the galley window. A man came out of the galley with a tray of china bowls.

Echohawk was hungry, but the soup bowl was so hot that he had to set it on the deck of the flatboat. All the soldiers leaned over the side to shout to some pretty girls who were standing on the riverbank. The flatboat tipped, and the soup bowl skidded along the deck. It crashed against the other side of the boat and broke. The soup splattered the wall.

The cook set another steaming bowl next to Echohawk's knee.

"We'll not let you go hungry, lad," the cook snarled as he shook his ladle at Echohawk. "But don't lose another."

Echohawk started to nod, then remembered that he was supposed to pretend not to understand English.

The hot soup smelled so good! He stretched out on his stomach and encircled his soup bowl with his bound arms. It was hard to wait until the soup was cool.

Echohawk put his lips to the bowl and slurped the soup. Red Fox did the same. They had to tilt the bowls with their bound hands to eat the meat and vegetables.

Soon after dusk they tied up in Albany. The city started at the riverbank and climbed all the way to the top of a steep hill. Yellow candlelight shone through hundreds and hundreds of windows.

Echohawk sat on deck and gasped in wonder, trying to take it all in.

"I have never seen so many buildings," he whispered in amazement. "It is as though I am seeing all the buildings I have ever seen in my whole life, all together. And more."

"How will we ever escape from such a place?" Red Fox whispered back. "There are people everywhere."

"The noise, Red Fox! Surely no one could hear us escaping."

Through the candlelit twilight they could see people, oxen, horses, dogs, and cats crowding the docks and streets. The horses whinnied and the oxen bellowed as loaded wagons thumped and groaned over the roads. People shouted to one another on the streets and through the doorways. Dogs barked at plump cats as they prowled around the docks.

Above the din the sound of men singing poured out of the low-lying buildings by the river. Every once in a while they'd stomp their feet together in time to the music.

And all along the riverbank there were logs, logs stacked as high as the buildings themselves. More flatboats, so laden with logs they were barely above the water, floated in midstream heading south. Abandoned logs floated aimlessly, bumping into the flatboats and clogging the river.

"So this is where the forest is going," Echohawk said. "They will cut it all down."

The captives watched the stars come out, and Red Fox called out the names of the constellations. "Now the Fox clan knows something is wrong," he said. "I should have been home by now."

He sank his head into his hands. In a few moments his shoulders were shaking. Echohawk heard rough sobs coming out of his friend whenever there was a lull in the music.

The soldiers sat in the galley and sang. Their songs became louder and louder as the night wore on. It was impossible to sleep.

Echohawk lay under the stars, shivering in the cold night air and listening to the soldiers sing and the little sisters cry.

In the morning Smoke Eyes and Fawn were gone. Echohawk wanted to ask what had happened but remembered Fawn's warning about not speaking any English.

Echohawk and Red Fox were given some bread, meat, and hot tea for morning corn. The sisters weren't given any food at all. The captives disembarked, and the soldiers marched them away from the lumber district. As they trudged up the steep hill, Echohawk glanced at the road marker—Tivoli Street. All along the way the streets were crowded with people who stared at the captives as they marched by.

The procession stopped in front of a grand brick house high on a hill overlooking the river. When Major Woodbridge knocked on the door, it was opened immediately by a soldier dressed in a bright red coat with gold braid on the collar.

The soldier who opened the door led them down a long hallway and into a large room. Soldiers stood at attention by the fireplace. Others guarded the door. They all held muskets at their sides. Like the townspeople outside, the soldiers stared hard at the captives.

An immense man sat behind a huge oaken desk. The man looked up as the captives stood at attention in front of him.

"The *patroon*," Echohawk whispered to Red Fox. "That must be him."

Patroon Henrick Van Rensselaer heaved himself up with his hands. A great fur cloak fell from his shoulders to his ankles. The cloak was made from hundreds of black squirrel skins.

"Patroon Henrick Van Rensselaer," Major Woodbridge said with a bow. "We have been on the Hudson as far north as the waterfall. These are the captives we've found this time."

The waterfall, Echohawk thought. *They've been in our camp!*

"Uncuff these boys, Major Woodbridge," the patroon commanded. "They're not prisoners. Indeed, their captivity is over."

"Yes, Patroon."

The patroon smiled at them as the major unlocked their handcuffs. Echohawk rubbed his sore wrists and licked the red spots where the iron had chafed them. Red Fox's thick wrists were raw and bleeding.

"Do any of you speak English?" the patroon said in a kindly voice. "Do you remember your mothers and fathers? Brothers? Sisters? Their names? Where they live?"

Major Woodbridge shoved Echohawk forward. "This one speaks English. At least he told us his name, Jonathan Starr. Some of my men have gone to Miss Starr's house to tell her."

Echohawk's eyes widened in shock. *Miss Starr?*

The patroon nodded to him. "Starr, is it?"

When Echohawk didn't say anything, Major Woodbridge shouted in his ear, "Answer the patroon!"

"Yes," Echohawk blurted out.

"Anyone else speak English? Any English at all?"

Silence.

The patroon tried again. *"Spreekt hier iemand nederlands?"*

Silence.

"Parlez-vous français?"

Silence.

The patroon sighed. "A sad business, Major. A sad business indeed. Neither English nor Dutch. Not even French."

"Yes, Patroon."

The little sisters stood apart from the others, holding hands and gawking at the richly carved furniture, the guards, the deep carpets, the paintings on the walls. Their blue eyes, opened wide with fear, reminded Echohawk of little Henry Watkins' eyes.

Patroon Henrick Van Rensselaer walked to the fireplace and lifted a glass jar from the mantelpiece. Inside the jar were brightly colored candies—red and white drops, green candy the color of spring leaves, bright red sticks, brown lumps of maple sugar. "You girls remember your mother and father, don't you?" he asked, wagging the jar of candy out toward them.

The hungry sisters pounced on the candy. They squealed and giggled as they stuffed more and more candy into their mouths.

"What are your names?" the patroon asked.

"Celia," the older girl mumbled through a mouthful of maple sugar.

"Celia's a pretty name. What's your little sister's name?"

"Sara!" the younger girl shouted through a mouth so stuffed with candy she looked like a chipmunk.

"Celia and Sara—such pretty names. Do you remember your last name? Your family name?"

"Tamaqua!" Celia shouted. She stuck out her tongue at her sister. Her tongue was bright green. Sara did the same. Her tongue was bright red. They giggled some more.

The patroon frowned.

"Patroon, *tamaqua* means 'beaver,'" Major Woodbridge explained. "It's a clan name among the Delaware. They must not remember their real family name."

Echohawk thought, *How does he know about clan names?*

Major Woodbridge stood in front of Echohawk and Red Fox. He smiled at them. "You have been away from your people for a long time," he said to them in perfect Munsee. "Some of you longer than others. Soon you will be with your own people again."

Echohawk and Red Fox stared at Major Woodbridge, as astonished as if a bear had started talking to them.

"Why—how—you speak our language! How—how do you know what to speak?" Red Fox sputtered in surprise.

Echohawk narrowed his eyes into yellow-brown slits. "He has understood everything we've said to each other. You talked to him, Red Fox. You did betray me."

Major Woodbridge smiled again. "Red Fox didn't have to say anything, Echohawk. You were walking on the riverbank, and I saw your brown hair.

"When I was a little older than the two of you, I lived on the long island among the Metoac. *Soldiers* rescued me, so I joined the *army*. You two have been plotting an escape." Major Woodbridge looked hard into Echohawk's eyes. "I escaped once and ran back to the Metoac. But *soldiers* found me, and I returned to the *army*. There I stayed. I knew where I belonged.

"There are many people on the earth, many different ways to live a life, little brothers. Soon you will return to your first life. It will be hard, but when you are older, like me, you will come to know that we were right to bring you here."

"You never saw your clan again?" Red Fox asked.

Major Woodbridge stood up straighter. "We will find your clan, Red Fox. Your real clan. With hair like a fox's back, they will not be hard to find."

"A boy with a build like his ought to become a farrier or even a lumberman," the patroon said in English. "Look at those arms, those shoulders. He was born to make horseshoes and nails. Ask around at the farrier's and blacksmith's shops down by the waterfront, Major. Perhaps someone will take him on as an apprentice while we look for his family. Meanwhile, we'll print the usual announcements in the newspapers for their parents."

"Yes, Patroon. Hayes, Turner, look sharp. Take this boy around to the ironworks shops in the lumber district. See if someone will take him on. If not, bring him back here."

Hayes and Turner each took an arm and led Red Fox away.

"Echohawk! Echohawk!" Red Fox's voice floated behind him as the soldiers pushed him into the hall.

"Red Fox! They are saying that you will make moccasins for *horses*," Echohawk called after him.

"Why?" he shouted back.

"I will see you again."

"Echohawk, if you see my parents again—"

The front door slammed shut with a bang.

"We should be able to find something for the three of you," Patroon Henrick Van Rensselaer said. He reached behind him and placed a large basket of toys on his desk.

"Little girls like dolls, don't they? Especially pretty ones."

The patroon held two dolls, dressed in pink and blue dresses, out to Celia and Sarah. The sisters snatched the dolls from his hands. They lay on their stomachs on the rug, playing with the dolls and eating from two big piles of candy.

"Mr. Starr?" The patroon held the toy basket out to him. "I see a slingshot in here."

Echohawk shook his head.

"Some candy, then? I've never met a boy who didn't like candy."

The patroon held out the glass jar and shook it. Echohawk looked away.

"Half of Glickihigan's advice was good advice," Major Woodbridge said in Munsee.

Echohawk glared at him. "Don't talk about my father."

"Pretend to be happy. As well you might, Echohawk. Fortune runs with you, because we know who you are. Most of the children we recover never see their real families again. These two sisters were stolen not so long ago, but surely their parents are dead. Their real parents, I mean."

Major Woodbridge shook his head. "They remember nothing, of course. They have blocked their parents' murder out of their minds. Perhaps the same thing has happened to you."

"My father is a trapper. So are you. But you trap hungry children with sweets and toys."

"I saw the Metoac kill my father, my mother, and my younger brothers. I was older than you are now. I remember everything," Major Woodbridge said bitterly. "I still have no idea why I was spared. I was taken back to their village. No clan wanted me, so I was a slave for the entire camp. It was 'Fishnet, do this' and 'Fishnet, do that' from sunrise until long after dark. If I can stop one captive from living as I did, then my parents and brothers did not die for nothing."

"I am not a slave," Echohawk replied. "And there are no Metoac left alive."

"The Metoac are . . . were a hard people," Major Woodbridge said softly. "They were whalers, seafarers. They cut my face, crisscrossed like a fishing net, so everyone would know I was only for work. I was fourteen winters when I was captured. I lived with the Metoac for five years."

"You escaped and went back to them."

"Jonathan? Jonathan Ethan Starr?"

A small woman with dark hair stood in the doorway. She was breathing hard, and her cheeks were bright red.

"Miss Starr," Major Woodbridge said, bowing. "I believe we have a relative here. Or so he says."

"I ran all the way up Tivoli Street," the woman replied. Her silk skirts rustled like the wind through bullrushes as she walked toward Echohawk. She placed her hands on the sides of his face.

Pretend to be happy. He did not jerk away from her.

"Jonathan? Is it really you, honey? I just don't know, Major Woodbridge," she cried. "I haven't seen him since he was four."

"He pretends not to know much English, Miss Starr," Major Woodbridge said. "Watch him very closely."

"Major Woodbridge, surely you are mistaken. Why would he pretend not to understand his own language?"

She stood right in front of Echohawk and stared hard into his face. He stared back.

"My brother's name was Ethan. Are you Ethan's boy?"

This close up, Echohawk saw that her dark hair was streaked with gray. Her eyes were the same yellow-brown color as his own.

He gasped, then so did she.

"Those eyes!" she shouted. "My brother's son. It's Jonathan!"

"Happy," Echohawk said in English. He glanced at Major Woodbridge, whose eyes had welled with tears.

"Of course you're happy, honey. Jonathan! It's a miracle!" Miss Starr threw her arms around his neck and started to cry.

"Miss Starr," Patroon Henrick Van Rensselaer said, "if you could take the little girls too? Celia and Sara. We believe they're sisters, and we'll make every effort to find their family."

"Of course I'll take them, the poor little things.

"Jonathan." She wiped her eyes with a lacy white

handkerchief. "I'm your Aunt Ruth. I know you don't remember me, honey. But you're home now. A miracle!"

"Happy," Echohawk said again.

Spirit-brother, spirit-helper, you tried to warn me. If only I could run as fast as you can fly.

Chapter Six

ICE

Miss Starr lived in a grand house on top of another hill.

As she fumbled with the door latch, tears welled up in her eyes. "Jonathan, if only your grandparents could have lived to see this day. You're home. Everything's going to be all right."

He was exhausted, the little sisters were bleary-eyed from lack of sleep, but Miss Starr didn't notice. The four of them went from room to room, Miss Starr prattling on excitedly.

Echohawk just smiled and said, "Thank you, thank you, thank you," every chance he had.

"Jonathan, look at this portrait—that's your great-great—oh, I don't know how many greats ago—grandfather, Comfort Starr. What a name for a doctor! The Starrs sailed to Massachusetts in 1635 on a ship called the *Hercules*. His son, Comfort Starr II, was one of the founders of Harvard. Have you heard of Harvard College?"

Echohawk stared hard at the painting.

Like a mirror, Red Fox had said to him in the Fox clan's wigwam. He saw his own yellow-brown eyes, his own reddish-brown hair, his own broad forehead and nose. But instead of the pleasure he had thought he would feel, sick horror washed over him.

Who am I?

A woman named Mildy, with a brown face and brown arms, cooked and served them noon corn. He was so hungry after the flatboat, and the little sisters too, that they ate everything Mildy put in front of them: ham and biscuits, applesauce, spiced peaches, chicken pies, venison pies, gingerbread with lemon sauce.

After noon corn Miss Starr made them each take a bath in the biggest stew pot Echohawk had ever seen. It was big enough to cook a person, or two people the size of Celia and Sara together.

He sat perfectly still as Mildy poured more and more hot water over his head.

Echohawk remembered his father telling him once about the brown people who lived among the English in the towns. They were slaves, just as Major Woodbridge had been a slave among the Metoac on the long island.

He said, "Thank you," again when Miss Starr

gave him breeches, boots, a soft white shirt, and a black wool coat to wear.

After changing into the strange clothes, he stood in front of a mirror and laughed merrily. The two sisters, Celia and Sara, also giggled, because except for the boots, everything was much too big.

"This too was your grandfather's," Miss Starr said to him. She placed a hat with the triangular shape of a cottonwood leaf on his head. The hat slid down around his ears. Everyone was laughing, Echohawk laughing the hardest.

But he was not laughing within his spirit, where it really mattered. He felt sore, scared, and hollow: like an oak cut down from her roots, dragged from her home in the forest, then scraped out to make a dugout canoe.

"I'll go into town tomorrow and engage a tailor, honey," Miss Starr said.

After evening corn Miss Starr showed him a room just for sleeping. The bed was stuffed with feathers and covered with blankets, just like the one he'd slept in at the Watkins'. The feather bed made a crunching sound when he lay down on it.

Echohawk thought of all the arrows that could have been fletched with these crushed feathers. Enough for everyone in the Munsee camp for years.

This room looked like the rest of Miss Starr's home. The bed, the table and chair, the cloths covering the windows, everything was covered with a spiderwebby cloth she called *lace*. Dried flowers in china vases, and more china, covered every surface.

Even if I had my tomahawk, knife, and Thunderpath, where could I have put them? he thought.

"Good night," he said to her. "Thank you, Aunt Ruth." And she started to cry.

He forced himself to stand still as she threw her arms around him once more. As she said good night, he smiled his biggest smile.

Except for the three nights of his Vision Quest, Echohawk had not spent one night of his life sleeping alone. He missed the usual snores, coughs, and rustling blankets. It was too quiet. All night long he kept waking up, wondering what was wrong, and then remembering.

❖ ❖ ❖

After morning corn Miss Starr bade him sit down near the fireplace, and she stood behind him. Echohawk thought she was going to unbraid his hair, then comb it for him, as his mother used to do long ago.

But before he knew what she was doing, she had cut his braids off.

Snip, snip.

And they were gone.

"No! No!" he screamed. He jumped up and spun around.

"My goodness," Miss Starr said, taking a step backward. "It's just hair."

"What have you done?"

His mother's comb had been carved from an elk's antler. Echohawk himself had placed it in her grave so that when he joined her in the next life, she could comb his hair there too. It had felt so good, so safe, sitting on the summer porch or in front of the starfire, his mother combing his long hair and telling him stories in her soft voice.

Sometimes at night Echohawk eased himself into sleep by pretending to feel her comb running through his hair and listening to her stories again.

Now his hair was gone. Miss Starr held the braids in her hands.

"I—I was just trying to help," she said. "It's unnatural for a man to have hair so long."

"What have you done?" he repeated.

He'd never had his hair cut. Never. Like every Mohican warrior's, Echohawk's hair was—had been—long enough for him to sit on.

"I'm sorry I've upset you." Miss Starr tossed the long ropes into the fire. As the braids burned, they moaned and sighed like sorrowing spirits.

Tears leaked out of his eyes like sap out of a sugar maple tree. He couldn't stop them.

"Mother," he whispered.

Lately he'd been thinking that his mother was holding the ends of his braids as she walked softly behind him. It was her way of holding on to him from her next life. As tired as he was, Echohawk could almost feel his braids lifting and almost hear the soft footfalls behind his own. He believed she was helping him, helping them all, to ease the journey of the Turtle clan.

Now she had nothing to hold on to; Echohawk already felt her spirit drifting away from him.

As they moaned and sighed, the burning braids gave off an acrid, bitter smell. His nose, his lungs, his spirit, all were filled with its bitterness.

"It's just hair," Miss Starr said, her voice shaking. Celia and Sara stood close to Echohawk and patted his arms.

He sat by the fire and watched his braids flame up, then turn to ashes. Tears splashed onto his lap. How could he pretend to be happy now?

Glickihigan had once told him a story of when he, Glickihigan, was eight winters. Like the other boys his age, he had jumped into the Muhekunetuk every dawntime during the four winter moons. Glickihigan's father had watched as his son chopped a hole in the ice. Glickihigan jumped in, then scrambled out.

Afterward Glickihigan had to walk all the way back to his mother's wigwam, where his clothes were placed next to the starfire, his hair as frozen and as stiff as a sheet of birch bark. His father said his teeth would be chattering like a turtle-shell rattle. He wouldn't warm up again until after noon corn.

Then at the next dawntime he jumped in all over again.

But jumping through the ice every day made him as

hard and still as the ice itself. Glickihigan is so tough, he can endure anything and not degrade himself by crying in front of strangers.

He'd wanted Echohawk to jump into the Muhe-kunetuk during the winter moons, but Echohawk had said no. His eighth winter was the coldest in anyone's memory; even the waterfall had frozen solid. This last winter was Bamaineo's eighth, but he'd spent the four winter moons in school instead. Now it was too late for both of them.

How I wish I'd said yes! If I were as tough as Glickihigan, Miss Starr could cut my braids and my mother away from me and throw them into the fire, and as they moaned and sighed like sorrowing spirits, my face would be as hard and cold and still as ice.

CHAPTER SEVEN
HANNAH

Eighteen suns went by and there was no sign of Glickihigan and Bamaineo. The sun kicked off his night blanket earlier and earlier, and the daylight was filled with sharp light and warm wind.

When no one was looking, Echohawk watched out his bedroom window, which faced the street, but he saw no one he recognized. Once, just as the edges softened into twilight, he thought he saw two figures dart behind the house across the street. He stared and stared until the house melted into the blackness, but he saw no other movement.

While he waited, Miss Ruth Starr's dressmaker came to call and made the little sisters pink and blue dresses with lots of ruffles and flounces. Miss Starr bought them pretty stockings and beribboned caps for their hair. The cobbler came to call and made girls' shoes, as thin and delicate as fallen leaves. Celia and Sara looked just like the dolls the Patroon had given them.

A tailor came to call and made Echohawk breeches, a shirt with a cravat trimmed in lace, and a jacket so long it brushed against his knees. What hair was left he tied back with a black ribbon.

He was used to walking silently. Now his booted feet clomped on the floorboards.

He hated the lacy cravat. It was scratchy and too tight. He felt tangled in the spider web of Miss Starr's lace, trapped tighter and tighter the more he struggled for freedom.

The only good thing was Miss Starr's pretty little brown mare, Hannah. Echohawk went into the stable behind the house anytime he could get away. He always had a treat for the horse—a pinch of salt, an apple core, carrot stubs, some molasses he'd poured on his palm for her to lick. Hannah would toss her head and nicker at him as he opened the stable door.

She was shedding her winter coat, and Echohawk brushed and brushed her until the long hair fell out. Her smooth spring coat gleamed like copper in the lamplight. Her black mane and tail sparkled like a raven's wings.

Echohawk placed the clumps of horsehair in the paddock so the birds could use it for nest building.

"Where are my father and brother, Hannah?" Echohawk would ask her again and again. He pressed his forehead against her neck. "How am I supposed to escape if I don't know where to go?"

Hannah nuzzled her nose into his shoulder, and he felt her warm, sweet breath in his ear.

❖ ❖ ❖

"I have been thinking about a college near Boston," Miss Starr said two evenings later at the dinner table. "It's late in the term, but they might take you."

Echohawk sat very still. "I went to school," he said.

Miss Starr smiled down the table at him. "There's more to school than just learning English, Jonathan. There are any number of things a gentleman should know: mathematics, history, geography, Latin and Greek."

"Jonathan in school, Jonathan in school," Celia chanted.

"Miss Celia is going to school too," Miss Starr announced. "There's a day school just for young ladies here in Albany. A dame school."

"I don't want to go to school," Celia said.

"Celia in school," Sara teased.

"Miss Sara will be going to school as well," Miss Starr replied briskly. "You girls are going to learn how to be ladies."

Echohawk put his spoon down. "There is no school here?" he asked softly. "In Albany?"

"None good enough for my only nephew."

"When?"

"As soon as possible," Miss Starr replied. "I'll write to them in the morning. I'll miss you, honey, but you'll be back for the summer holidays."

He stood up so hard his chair fell back. "I clean Hannah's clothes now."

Mildy came out of the kitchen with a steaming apple pie.

"Not clothes," Miss Starr said, laughing.

"What did you say, Miss Starr?" Mildy asked.

"Horses don't wear clothes, Jonathan, they wear tack or harness."

"What?" Mildy asked again.

Miss Starr sighed. "Please excuse me, children. Mildy is as deaf as a post."

She turned to Mildy. "He said 'clothes' instead of 'tack' . . . for a horse," she shouted.

"Clothes for a horse? I'm not washin' no clothes for a horse, Miss Starr," Mildy replied defiantly.

Miss Starr rested her head wearily in her hands. "That's not what I said."

"Clothes for a horse!" Celia shrieked.

The little sisters laughed so hard, cider ran out of their noses. They leaned back, then screamed as their chairs fell backward, dumping them to the floor.

"Girls, girls!" Miss Starr shouted. "We are ladies!"

In the confusion Echohawk ducked out the back door and ran into the stable.

"Hannah, what will I do?" he asked, his face buried in her warm neck. "*Boston!* The Turtle clan will never find me there. What will I do?" He took a deep breath. "What if they have already left without me?"

Hannah rested her head on his shoulder and sighed.

❊ ❊ ❊

Two or three times a week Miss Starr took her carriage to town. Echohawk watched closely as she buckled Hannah into the breastplate, bridle, reins, and traces. It looked like hard work, so he began to help her. Then one morning he hitched Hannah to the carriage all by himself.

"Jonathan, thank you so much, honey."

"You are welcome, Aunt Ruth."

He helped Miss Starr step into the driver's box as the little sisters clambered into the backseat.

"Come with us today," Miss Starr said.

"Yes, come with us, Jonathan," Sara said.

Echohawk shook his head. His aunt always invited him, and he always said no. What if Glickihigan were watching at this very moment? He could escape while Aunt Ruth was in town!

"I need your help, Jonathan. Hannah needs your help. What with all the rain last night, the mud will be fearsome today."

"All right." As Echohawk sat down next to her, Miss Starr touched Hannah's right side with her whip.

"Walk on, Hannah," Miss Starr called out.

Hauling the carriage behind her, Hannah began to walk from the very top of Pearl Street down to the broad Market Street and the lumber district. Pearl Street was a corduroy road—held in place with logs stacked like a steep staircase.

It was a brisk spring day. The sun felt warm, but the wind blew cold against Echohawk's face. Women swept front stoops or walked in twos or threes down the steep sidewalk toward the riverbank. Men tacked up their horses to carriages and shouted greetings to neighbors. Children, schoolbooks bound together with leather straps and slung over their shoulders, dragged their heels over the log sidewalk.

"Your father wanted to be a pioneer," Miss Starr was saying as her jolting carriage lurched down the steep hill. Every time the carriage wheels crashed over a log in the road, Echohawk squeezed the handbrake so hard that the veins on his arm stood out.

"Easy, Hannah. Don't slip in the mud, honey," she called out in a brave voice as Hannah slipped and skidded down the hill.

"Spring showers," she said, half to herself. Hannah was breathing hard; her flanks heaved in and out, in and out.

Slip, thud, slip, thud—all the way down the hill.

"I had a perfectly good house just waiting for him on Pearl Street, but oh, no, your father wanted to be a pioneer.

"Pioneering cost your father his life," she said grimly, "and the life of your mother and your darling brothers and sister."

Slip, thud, slip, thud.

Echohawk glanced behind him. "Celia and Sara, you are all right?" he asked. The sisters gripped hard at the carriage railings and for once weren't getting into mischief.

"I—I think so," Celia replied.

"Celia was your mother's name." Miss Starr looked at Echohawk sharply. "Jonathan, do you remember your own mother?"

"Celia Starr," he said slowly. "No, I do not remember her."

Hannah tried to kick her back legs in the air. Echohawk saw her ears go back as she strained to break away from her harness. He wanted to speak softly to her, to reassure her as her legs sank into the deep, sticky mud. If only Aunt Ruth would stop talking for a moment!

"That's too bad. Before your father left, I said to him, and I remember it as though it were yesterday, I said, 'Ethan, you might as well tomahawk my beautiful niece and nephews right now, because if you think upriver is safe—'"

Miss Starr gave the reins a shake. "No, Hannah, bad girl, bad Hannah. Hannah, walk on." Hannah had stopped in front of the downtown inn and would not take another step. The horse lifted her ears expectantly and looked toward the inn's front door. She whinnied and scraped at the mud with her right front hoof.

"Hannah, walk on," Miss Starr ordered. "Walk on."

"I pull Hannah, Aunt Ruth?" Echohawk said.

"No, Jonathan, that won't do any good; she's already stopped. At least we're down the hill," she said in a grateful voice.

"Mr. Roberts," she called out. "Mr. Roberts, it's Hannah!"

A curtain rustled in the inn's front window. A man stepped out the door and walked briskly down the stone steps. He held a bunch of carrots in one hand. Hannah nodded her head and nickered.

"You've spoiled her, Mr. Roberts," Miss Starr scolded, but there was a smile on her face. "She won't go any farther without her treat."

Mr. Roberts held out a carrot half in the palm of his hand.

"Spoiled her, have I? Anytime you want to sell her, I'll be happy to spoil her some more." Hannah crunched the carrot, then pushed her nose against Mr. Roberts' chest for another. He gave her the second half and then a smaller carrot.

"There, Hannah," Mr. Roberts said in a soft voice. "Who's my favorite girl?" He stroked her nose.

"You know I'd never sell Hannah, Mr. Roberts. She's like one of the family.

"Speaking of family, this is my nephew, Jonathan Ethan Starr. He's been living with the savages since he was a baby. Imagine!"

"Good morning to you, Mr. Starr." Mr. Roberts held out his hand. "Welcome home."

Echohawk forced himself to smile. "Good morning, Mr. Roberts."

Mr. Roberts' hand felt warm from Hannah's breath and smelled sweet from the carrots. He had an enormous red nose, and his gray hair and beard formed a complete circle around his face.

As Echohawk studied Mr. Roberts, Mr. Roberts studied him.

"He looks like you, Miss Starr. He has those same sharp eyes, the same nose and chin."

"Yes, he does." Miss Starr said, putting her hand on Echohawk's arm. "And he's been such a help to me: pumping water, chopping firewood, helping me take care of Hannah. He's wonderful with Hannah, and she is devoted to him. Jonathan taught himself how to hitch her to the carriage just by watching me."

"Those Indians think animals have spirits . . . souls, just like people do. Smart lad." Mr. Roberts' eyes twinkled. "I'll buy the both of them."

"Oh, you're impossible! Good day to you, Mr. Roberts. Walk on, Hannah."

"Miss Starr," Mr. Roberts said seriously, taking hold of Hannah's bridle. "Never take your eyes off this boy, not even for a moment. As soon as your back is turned, as soon as you let down your defenses, he'll leave. I've seen it happen time and time again."

Echohawk studied Hannah's swishing tail and pretended not to understand what Mr. Roberts was saying. His heart began to pound, his face to burn.

"What nonsense! Why would he leave now that he's home again?"

"Surely you don't think he's been living all by himself, out in the wilderness?"

Miss Starr gathered the reins in her hands.

"He has an Indian family out there in the woods, an Indian family waiting for him to return," Mr. Roberts said. "The patroons and the Crown have been paying ransoms for about a year now. I can't tell you how many captives and their families I've seen in my inn. The families are overjoyed to have their sons and daughters back, but the captives are miserable and always, *always* try an escape."

Aunt Ruth put her hand on Echohawk's arm. "Where is your Indian family?" she asked slowly.

Echohawk waited for a moment before speaking. "They are gone," he said in a slow, sad voice.

"What do you mean they're gone? They're dead?"

"Gone, Aunt Ruth."

"You've nowhere to go? Is that what you're telling me?"

"They are gone, Aunt Ruth."

"There's your answer, Mr. Roberts. They're gone. Gone and good riddance."

Mr. Roberts shook his head. "Miss Starr, captive children change completely. They become Indian, completely Indian. Never take your eyes off him for a moment."

"Jonathan's happy. He's told me so himself, at

88

Patroon Henrick Van Rensselaer's own house,"
Miss Starr said angrily. "No more carrots today,
Hannah. Walk on."

Miss Starr touched her whip to Hannah's right
side, and the horse began to walk again.

"Good day to you, Mr. Roberts," she called
behind her. "Hannah, trot on."

As Hannah trotted toward the shops, Echohawk
sat bolt upright in the carriage box. Just in front of
them two men were leaning against a building, eye-
ing Hannah. Their heads were plucked clean save
for one strip down the center.

"Mohawks," he whispered. Instinctively he held
one hand in front of his aunt to protect her.

"That's the Indian House, honey. It's a house for
trappers and traders; some come from as far away as
Canada. Sort of an inn just for the Indians. They
won't hurt us."

The Indian House was an odd mix of Iroquois
longhouse and English farmhouse. The walls and
roof were made of bark, but there were glass windows in the front and a door made of planked wood.

The Mohawks, one short, the other tall, stood in
the front yard as the carriage went by. Echohawk
studied them, his heart in his throat. Mohawks and
Mohicans, like two bears who meet in the forest, had
been enemies longer than anyone could remember.

As the Mohawks watched Hannah closely, Echohawk looked them over quickly for weapons. They
paid no attention to him.

Of course, these Mohawks have no idea who I am.

Miss Starr pulled Hannah to a stop in front of a ladies' dressmaking shop, and Echohawk helped her out of the carriage. He looked in the window. The tiny shop was full of elegant ladies sitting on delicate furniture. They all had little dogs in their laps. Bolts of silk, wool, and lace were stacked neatly against the silk-covered walls.

The little sisters spotted two child-size silk caps in the shop window. They began to jump up and down around Miss Starr.

"Jonathan, I know you don't want to go in there." Miss Starr smiled at him. "Even though all my friends so want to meet you. I'll have an afternoon tea party soon. They can meet you then."

"Please, please, Miss Starr?" Celia and Sara pointed to the lacy pink caps and tugged at her coat sleeves.

"We'll see about the bonnets. But you girls definitely need gloves. A lady's hands should be snow white, and your hands are as brown as any Indian's."

She pressed some coins into Echohawk's palm. "Here, honey. The bakery is across the street. Buy yourself a treat. We won't be more than a moment."

CHAPTER EIGHT
PLANS

Echohawk wandered across the street to the bakery, dodging carts and carriages all the way.

He groaned. A tea party! It didn't take much imagination to figure out what a tea party was. Sitting in Aunt Ruth's lacy parlor in stiff, scratchy clothes, while the ladies twittered like birds and fed little cakes to their lapdogs.

A Mohican warrior at a tea party!

"Glickihigan, where are you?" he muttered.

He wanted to shout, to scream for help. *Maybe there are Delaware in the Indian House. I could run there and back if I hurry. I'll ask them if they've seen my father and brother. If nothing else, I could hide among them when they leave Albany. Perhaps they have a spare breechcloth, an extra pair of leg-*

gings for a disguise. I could trade these boots for moccasins.

He turned in the direction of the Indian House, but a pile of doughnuts in the bakery window caught his eye. Echohawk swallowed hard at the tight lump in his throat.

"Bamaineo," he whispered, his eyes filling with tears. "Here are your *doughnuts*."

Someone laughed behind him.

"Will you get me a *doughnut*, Echohawk?"

He whirled around.

"Bamaineo! Where did you come from?"

"When can you escape? We have been waiting for you."

Echohawk drew his brother into the alley between the bakery and a tavern.

"Where is Glickihigan?"

"He is trading his furs for supplies. He is there." Bamaineo pointed to a trading post down the street.

"We have seen Red Fox, too. Rather, I have," Bamaineo said importantly. "I saw him making moccasins for *horses*. There." Bamaineo pointed to a farrier's shop down the street. "I waved to Red Fox, but he didn't see me. You look funny in those clothes, Echohawk, like a trickster."

"Bamaineo, tell our father I am here, waiting for him. Tell him I do not have much time."

"Time for *doughnuts*?"

"Go!"

Echohawk took off his tricornered hat and

pressed his back against the wall. In no time Glickihigan was in the alley too.

"Father—"

"Come." Glickihigan took him by the elbow and led him farther away from the street.

Glickihigan cupped his hands around Echohawk's face.

"I am so proud of you."

"I thought you were gone!" Echohawk burst into tears. He turned his back in embarrassment and pressed his forehead against the side of the tavern.

His father and brother waited patiently for him to stop crying. Echohawk angrily wiped his face with his sleeves.

"I told you we would never leave without you," his father said.

"But I haven't seen you or heard from you," Echohawk cried out. The tavern was made of rough logs, the bark still clinging in places. The bits of bark pressed into his hot forehead.

"Shhh—she will see your tear-stained face and know something is wrong," Glickihigan said softly. "She is no longer watching you? Surely we can leave soon."

"She already knows something is wrong," Echohawk said, his face still pressed to the wall. "This is not the first time I have disgraced myself with tears."

"What happened to your hair, Echohawk?" Bamaineo asked.

"It will grow back," Glickihigan said quickly. "We have been watching you all this time. We saw the soldiers take Red Fox away and the woman take you and her daughters away. We saw you helping her and her daughters step inside the *carriage* this morning. We saw the man feeding the *horse* carrots and heard his warning. I am proud of you for keeping your face so still."

"But I have not kept my face still. She cut my hair . . ." Echohawk sobbed.

"Ice!" he whispered fiercely to himself. "As hard and cold and still as ice."

He wiped his face with his sleeve again, took a deep breath, and turned around.

"She wants to send me to Boston for *school*. Right away."

"More *school?*" Bamaineo exclaimed.

"We have to leave now," Echohawk said, wiping his face with his sleeve again.

Glickihigan thought for a moment, then shook his head. "You can't escape now, not in the daylight, not so close to the *carriage*, and not with so many *soldiers* by the river. We will leave in the dawntime tomorrow. Can you steal away then? We will meet north of *Albany* in the oak-tree grove. Wear these English clothes. No one will notice you if you wear them."

"I can get away. She sleeps well into the morning. But she has a slave who is awake in the dawntime." Echohawk thought for a moment. "This brown-faced

94

slave does not hear well. She won't notice me leaving."

Bamaineo's mouth dropped open. "She does not hear well because she has a brown face?"

"No, little brother, that's not the reason."

Bamaineo tugged at Glickihigan's sleeve. "I want to see her face. Echohawk, her ears are brown, too?"

"I have not seen her ears, little brother. She wears a sort of blanket around her head."

Bamaineo's mouth was as round as a doughnut. "Father, I want to see—"

Glickihigan put his hand over Bamaineo's mouth.

"Tomorrow, then. If you are not in the oak-tree grove, we will be there for the next dawntime and the next. We will not leave without you."

"Bamaineo saw Red Fox."

"He can leave with us. But he will have to go to the Munsee camp by himself. It is too dangerous for you to go back there. Return now, before the woman becomes more suspicious."

"I will be there tomorrow."

"Before the sun kicks off his night blanket. Go."

"Do you like wearing the *boots*, Echohawk?"

He smiled down at his little brother. "They hurt my feet, Bamaineo. They are heavy and splash the mud."

He gave Glickihigan the coins his aunt had given him. "My little brother has been asking about *doughnuts* again. . . . Father, her name is Starr. Ruth Starr."

A faint flicker of surprise lit up his father's eyes. "Talk to Red Fox now," Glickihigan said.

※ ※ ※

Echohawk stood in front of the farrier's shop watching Red Fox. His friend was wearing his regular leggings and breechcloth but no shirt. His red hair was in one long braid down his back.

The muscles in his thick arms and heavy chest gleamed with sweat. *He should be Red Bear, not Red Fox*, Echohawk thought. Red Fox was pounding on a flat, black stone with something that looked like a war club. Behind him was a bed of white-hot coals.

"No, no!" A man even bigger than Red Fox was shouting at him from the rear of the shop. Red Fox either couldn't hear him or was pretending he couldn't.

As Echohawk entered, smoke and steam filled his nose and lungs. On the flat black stone lay a horseshoe, glowing cherry red. Red Fox's face was almost as red as the horseshoe.

"Echohawk!" Red Fox stopped pounding.

"No, boy, no!" the man shouted, running toward Red Fox. "Always strike while the iron is hot." The man glared at Echohawk. "Who are you?"

"His friend," Echohawk replied in English.

Red Fox started pounding the horseshoe again.

"Tell your friend his horseshoes are terrible.

They're too thick and lumpy. A horse would go lame wearing those shoes."

"Lumpy? Lame? I don't know these words."

"They're not smooth," the big man shouted impatiently. "A horse would never walk again in the horseshoes he makes."

"Red Fox," Echohawk shouted above the din. "This man says your *horseshoes* are not thin enough. And not smooth enough. You will make a *horse* crippled and in pain."

"What does that have to do with me?" Red Fox shouted back.

Echohawk thought about Hannah's soft, trusting eyes and the way she nuzzled her nose into the crook of his arm when she wanted her neck scratched.

Two horses stood tied up in the aisle, waiting patiently to be shod.

Echohawk said, "Red Fox, if you make smooth *horseshoes*, this man will stop watching you."

Red Fox picked up the glowing horseshoe with a pair of pincers and dipped it into a water bucket. Steam hissed through the air.

"Smoke Eyes was right," he said through clenched teeth. "They never stop watching."

"Do you remember Celia and Sara, the little sisters? They are living with me in Ruth Starr's *house*. She says she is my aunt. I believe her."

Red Fox began pounding the horseshoe again.

"No, boy, no!" the man shouted. "It's too cold now."

The man pushed Red Fox out of the way and put the horseshoe back into the white-hot coals.

"I like my own little sisters better," Red Fox muttered.

"What happened to your foxtail necklace?" Echohawk asked.

Red Fox jerked his thumb toward the farrier. "He made me take it off."

"Good news, Red Fox. I leave tomorrow. My father and brother are here. We'll meet in the dawntime, before the sun kicks off his night blanket. Join us—north, in the oak-tree grove."

"I will be there," Red Fox replied eagerly. "I knew you'd think of a way for us to escape."

The farrier pushed Red Fox aside, placed the white-hot horseshoe on the anvil, and began pounding it. Red Fox walked to the back of the shop and dipped a tin cup into a barrel of water. He took a long, deep drink and then another.

"There," the farrier said. "Now there's a horseshoe. Boy!" he shouted. "You're supposed to be watching me."

Red Fox dipped the tin cup into the barrel and took another long drink.

"What's that good-for-nothing boy's name?" the farrier shouted to Echohawk, even though he was standing right next to him.

Echohawk thought for a moment. "He Is As Red As a Fox," he replied in English.

The big man scratched his head. "What kind of a name is that?" He pointed to a spot next to him. "Come here! Your name is John!" he bellowed at Red Fox. "John Smith. That's my name, too. Come here! Now!"

Red Fox angrily flung the tin cup aside. It bounced along the floorboards and landed in a pile of horse manure.

"No, boy, no!"

Echohawk backed out of the farrier's shop. He heard the man yelling at Red Fox from far down the street.

CHAPTER NINE
THE TRUTH

"Where have you been?" Aunt Ruth snapped.

Aunt Ruth and the little sisters were sitting in the carriage. Celia and Sara were wearing new gloves and the caps they'd seen in the dressmaker's window. They were eating cookies.

"I'm waiting for my answer." Aunt Ruth's face was pinched and hard, and her yellow-brown eyes had narrowed into angry slits. "You weren't in the bakery. You weren't in the street. I have to know where you've been, Jonathan."

Just beyond her shoulder, Echohawk saw his father and brother. They were standing in the doorway of the Indian House watching him.

"Hannah needs horseshoes?" he said, pointing down the street to the farrier's where Red Fox was working. "I asked the man there."

His aunt's face changed.

"Hannah doesn't need new horseshoes, honey. I was worried about you. Don't run off again, you hear?"

"Horseshoes are bad there, Aunt Ruth. They will hurt her."

"My farrier comes to the house, Jonathan. Every six weeks. Don't wander off again, do you hear me?"

"Yes, Aunt Ruth." Echohawk stepped into the carriage.

Miss Starr gave the reins a snap, and they began the slippery climb home.

Echohawk and the little sisters got out of the carriage as Hannah hauled it up Pearl Street. Hannah looked right at him, her eyes filled with panic and fear. She began to pant, and her flanks streaked with frothy sweat. Whenever she tried to stop and catch her breath, the carriage would start to slide down the muddy hill and thump over the logs. She tried to rear up; her front legs flailed at the air.

Aunt Ruth sat in the driver's box, back straight, elbows in. Her lips stretched into a smile.

"I am sorry, Hannah," Echohawk said softly. "You have to work so hard, and we could have easily walked into town this morning."

Just as Hannah began to stop, Echohawk would pull on her bridle to guide her forward. He spoke to her gently all the way home.

Once they were in the carriage house, he unhitched the panting mare and led her to her stall. To cool her down, Echohawk rubbed her legs and chest with a clean cloth soaked with water and mint oil. When Hannah's flanks were no longer heaving, he gave her hay, oats, and water.

By the time he was in the house, his muddy boots by the door, afternoon tea was ready.

Every afternoon it was the same: little cakes, ginger cookies, lemonade for the girls, tea with milk and sugar for Aunt Ruth and himself. They were expected to talk to one another while balancing little dishes on their knees. Mildy stood by the tea table and kept Miss Starr's teacup full.

The food was good, and the tea refreshing, but why they had to sit in the parlor for so long just to eat was a complete and utter mystery.

"Jonathan, I have a question for you."

"Yes, Aunt Ruth?"

Miss Starr sat up straight and watched him closely.

"Who were those people, those Indians, you were talking with?"

His legs jerked. The little plate of cookies on his lap clattered to the floor.

"I—I spoke to no one."

"Miss Celia has been talking to me while you were in the carriage house. She said an Indian boy approached you, the two of you spoke briefly, then he ran off and returned with an old Indian. The old Indian led you down the alley between the bakery and the Blue Goose Tavern. Only then did you go— alone—to the farrier's. Who were those people?"

"I don't . . . I don't understand what you say."

"You understand everything I say," Aunt Ruth replied tartly. "Who were they?"

"I talked to no one, Aunt Ruth."

"I see." Miss Starr paused for a moment. "Then where are my coins?"

Echohawk put his teacup on the table. He quickly placed his hands in his lap so his aunt wouldn't see how hard they were shaking. The little sisters crawled around his feet, squealing as they pounced on his fallen cookies.

"That's mine! That's mine!"

"No, Sara, that's mine!"

"Coins?" Echohawk asked.

"I meant for you to spend them at the bakery, but you didn't go to the bakery. Where are my coins?" Miss Starr held her hand out to him. "My coins, please."

Echohawk stared at his hands, his mind racing to think of an excuse for the missing coins.

"Jonathan in trouble," Celia called out from the floor in a playful voice.

"Girls, get up at once," Aunt Ruth said crossly. "You'll muss your dresses."

Celia and Sara sat down across from him and munched ginger cookies. Their bright eyes were dancing with mischief as they drummed their heels against their chairs.

"I bought doughnuts, Aunt Ruth."

"You weren't in the bakery."

"I went to another bakery."

"There is no other bakery." Miss Starr snapped her napkin down upon the table. "Out with it, Jonathan. The truth. I don't appreciate being lied to at my own tea table."

Echohawk stole a glance in his aunt's direction. Her face was as white as salt, her eyes lit with cold fury.

"I'm waiting," she said. "We'll sit here forever if need be."

The clock ticked, the fire hissed and sputtered. Even the little sisters were quiet.

Panicked thoughts zigzagged through his mind. It was hard to breathe.

What can I say? What can I say to throw her off my trail?

But he knew, just as a rabbit knows when there is no escape, that his aunt would never stop watching him now.

"Celia and Sara like to play tricks," he murmured.

"Who's playing tricks?" his aunt asked.

Echohawk switched to his own language. "Little sisters," he said bitterly, "that was my father and brother, and now I will never see them again because of you."

"What did you say to them?" Aunt Ruth shouted as Celia and Sara began to cry.

"I'm happy, Aunt Ruth—"

"Come with me."

Aunt Ruth took Echohawk by the arm, marching him up the stairs and down the hall toward his bedroom. She pushed him into the center of the room. Celia and Sara tagged after them.

"You have one more chance," she said, her arms across her chest. "The truth, Jonathan."

He sat on the bed and stared at the floor. "I—I spoke to no one."

"I see," his aunt said. "Mr. Roberts was right, wasn't he? You do intend to leave as soon as my back is turned. I've tried hard to make you happy, and I'm very sorry I haven't succeeded. More than you know. But that doesn't mean I don't know what's best for you. Come, girls."

Aunt Ruth pushed the girls into the hallway. Celia poked her head around the doorframe.

"Jonathan, I'm sorry!"

Aunt Ruth pulled Celia away from the door and slammed it behind her. The latch made an odd clicking sound.

Echohawk waited until he was sure his aunt was downstairs before he rolled his deerskin clothes into a bundle. Then he sat on the bed to wait.

I'll leave when night falls. Perhaps Glickihigan and Bamaineo are already at the oak-tree grove, waiting for me. We could have a full night of walking before she discovers I am missing.

Red Fox! I'll have to go to the riverbank and find him.

He thought about saying farewell to Hannah but decided against it. His aunt might hear her nickering and come out to investigate.

Echohawk lay down on the bed and tried to rest.

The light was fading as he looked around his room for the last time.

My aunt says she knows what's best for me. But she doesn't even know who I am. This is her home; this is her life. I could never live here.

❂ ❂ ❂

Echohawk placed one of his prized possessions, a hawk's red tail feather, on his pillow.

"Thank you for your kindness, Aunt Ruth," he whispered.

With his ear at the crack under the door, Echohawk listened for sounds on the stairway and in the front hall. His sharp ears picked up the soft tread of feet on the stairs, of doors closing softly. After waiting for what seemed like forever, he heard no sounds in the house.

They're sleeping. Good-bye, Aunt Ruth.

Echohawk pulled at the door handle.

The door didn't open.

He tried again. Again. He pulled with all his strength.

Echohawk hid his deerskin clothes under the bed.

"Aunt Ruth?" he called out. "The door is wrong—broken. Aunt Ruth? Aunt Ruth?" he called out, louder.

Footsteps in the hall.

"Your door's locked, Jonathan."

"What means 'locked'?"

"That means it won't open until I open it from this side."

Echohawk pulled again on the door handle. *Locked.* Cold horror washed over him. *It can't be true.*

"Aunt Ruth!" he shouted, pounding on the door. "Aunt Ruth!" He pulled and twisted the handle, but the door wouldn't budge.

"Aunt Ruth, Aunt Ruth!"

He rushed to the window and snapped it open. Cool night air rushed in, filling his nose with the scent of freedom. But the window was too high. He couldn't jump without hurting himself.

"Aunt Ruth! I'll tell the truth now."

"No, you won't. Good night, Jonathan."

"Aunt Ruth!"

❈ ❈ ❈

The stars were fading when the door opened softly.

Echohawk sprang to his feet. It was Mildy, holding a candle and a key in one hand, and putting a finger to her lips with the other. Under her arm was a cloth, the edges tied up into a bundle.

"Hush, Mr. Starr," she whispered. "Everyone t' house all asleep. You take this poke, go out to the wilderness. You be free with your folks."

Mildy gave him the bundle of cloth. Echohawk untied the ends and saw ginger cookies and a part of a ham studded with cloves.

Mildy shook her head. "Lock *you* up, what she thinkin'? Might as well lock up the wind."

"Why are you letting me go?" Echohawk whispered.

"I hear some, Mr. Starr, but not much." Mildy pointed to his mouth. "But I see you talkin'. I see what folks say. When I preten' I don't hear what folks say, they say a whole lot more." Mildy studied his face. "Maybe you know 'bout that for the same reason?"

"Aunt Ruth will be angry with you."

Mildy nodded to the hawk feather on the pillow. "I tell Miss Starr a hawk freed you. Took you away on broad brown wings."

Echohawk gasped. "You are my hawk?"

She nodded toward the door. "Go on, go out an' be free in the wilderness with your folks."

He tried again. "You are my spirit-helper?"

Mildy smiled at him. "What a nice thing t' say. Hurry, now."

Echohawk and Mildy crept down the stairs. When Echohawk opened the front door, he turned to speak to her.

"Say good-bye to Hannah for me."

She nodded.

"Tell Celia I forgive her for telling Miss Starr about my father and brother."

Mildy made a face. "Wild as Indians, those girls. Oh." Her hand flew to her mouth. "I beg your pardon, Mr. Starr."

Echohawk's face broke into a wide grin. He put

on his boots. "Thank you, Mildy," he said, shutting the door.

❖ ❖ ❖

In the dawntime there were a few people about, but his father had been right. No one even looked at him, dressed like everyone else.

Glickihigan and Bamaineo were waiting for him in the oak-tree grove, about halfway up a hill just north of town.

"Red Fox is coming too," Echohawk told them.

"We can't wait much longer, my son," Glickihigan replied. "The eastern sky becomes streaked with light. She will be looking for you."

"He will be here, Father."

As they waited, a slice of bright-red sun came over the steep eastern bank of the Muhekunetuk. More and more people crowded the streets.

"We will go now," Glickihigan said. "Now."

"But Red Fox said he would be here."

"You told him we would leave before the sun kicks off his night blanket?"

"Yes, but—"

"Then he knows we are gone."

Glickihigan turned on his heel and began climbing. Bamaineo followed.

Echohawk looked down at Albany. The town was waking up, people hurrying down the streets to the marketplace. Already lumbermen were stacking logs onto flatboats. There were soldiers everywhere.

He heard the faint chink, chink, chink from the farrier's and blacksmith's shops that lined the riverbank.

"Good-bye, Hannah, good-bye, Red Fox," he whispered. "Good-bye, Aunt Ruth."

❈ ❈ ❈

"She really is my aunt, Father," Echohawk said at the campfire that night. The ham studded with cloves, ginger cookies, and cold fresh water had made a good evening corn. There was none left.

All day they had hurried south. Now they were in the foothills of the Catskills. It was colder up here than on the riverbank. The Turtle clan huddled in bearskins.

Glickihigan looks tired, Echohawk thought, *and we've only just started our journey to the Three Sisters.*

"Her face looks just like mine. The same face but such a different life."

"Your brother and I never saw her husband."

"She has no husband. I think she has never had one. She has a *horse* named Hannah. I will miss her. Hannah has the spirit of a gentle girl."

"But the woman has daughters, your cousins."

"Celia and Sara are not her daughters. They were captured by the soldiers, as I was."

"She will miss you, then."

"She wanted me to go to *Boston* and learn something called *Latinandgreek*. What is that?"

"Languages white men spoke a long time ago."

"Then why do they learn them?"

"Part of their history, part of who they are."

"I see." Echohawk poked at the campfire with a stick.

Glickihigan hesitated. "You regret leaving your aunt?"

"No. She meant well. She really did. But our lives are as different as a trout and a hummingbird. Anyway"—Echohawk stirred the fire again—"I did not say good-bye to her."

"You should sleep. We really start climbing tomorrow. We will have to be very careful in Mohawk country—no mistakes because we are tired. Echohawk?"

"Yes?"

"You are gone. That is good-bye enough. If she thinks hard about why you have left, she will understand."

"The schoolmaster must have known about the *ransom*, but I never heard him speak of it. I never saw the gold in his eyes."

"He wanted you, not the gold."

"It is true about the Mohawks?" Echohawk asked softly, glancing in Bamaineo's direction. But his brother was already snoring in his bearskin. "Is it true they eat their prisoners?"

"I have heard this, but not from the Mohawks

themselves. They are a fierce people. Perhaps they want to be thought of as fiercer still."

Echohawk gave the campfire one last poke with his stick, then stretched out on his back. The night sky was filled with stars.

"The earth is a strange place," he said. "In *Albany* there are *bonnets, lace, lemonade, afternoon tea,* dried flowers, and sleeping platforms made of feathers. And on the other side of the mountains there are people who eat people."

"A strange place but a good place." Glickihigan took a deep breath. "You are wondering if I can walk to the Three Sisters. You wonder if I am strong enough."

"You are strong," Echohawk said quickly.

"But not strong enough, you think. I have never forgotten the first time I could do something better than my father. We were running along the river-bank and I beat him, without even trying. Just as you are feeling now, I felt sad and afraid."

"You always know what I'm thinking," Echohawk said softly.

"After that moment I could no longer admire my father without measure. It was as though I could see his shadow becoming smaller, right in front of my eyes," Glickihigan said. "I knew then that someday I would no longer be able to stand within his shadow. That's why I was sad. Someday I would have to stand alone. That's why I was afraid."

Echohawk shivered. "I see you panting for

breath. I see you rubbing your legs. I—I am afraid."

"I have walked to the Three Sisters and back again once this year. I can do it again. I have plenty of shadow left. Good night."

"Good night."

Later, a dream stirred Echohawk awake. It was Mildy, swooping down from the sky to rescue him. He sat astride her back as her broad brown arms flew him farther and farther into the forest. Mildy's arms turned to wings just as the scent of ham, cloves, and ginger filled his nose.

Echohawk sat up. The night was absolutely silent except for the steady beating of distant wings, becoming fainter and fainter in the darkness.

Chapter Ten
QUIET

The Turtle clan woke to a light blanket of snow. It dusted the bearskin blankets and the backpacks. The muskets, which lay within easy reach of Glickihigan and Echohawk, were also dusted with snow.

It was midspring, almost the end of the Dogwood Moon, but this far up the mountains the leaves on the trees were only as big as a squirrel's ear. The air was fresh and cold.

The tiny spring leaves swirled into a bright-green mist against the dark tree trunks and the pale dawn-time sky. Farther down the broad river valley, the shining green mist gave over to a denser and deeper green, as the full-leafed trees met the dark line of the Muhekunetuk.

A brisk wind blew off the Catskills. Echohawk

woke up stiff and shivering and knew he wouldn't be warm again until the Turtle clan started climbing.

They ate handfuls of new snow and strips of smoked venison for morning corn. They broke off tiny twigs of sassafras and chewed the green wood to get the morning taste out of their mouths.

As they chewed, they watched the sun rise slowly over the river valley below them. The sunlight played on the dark blue water. Sunbeams lit the curving river and flashed into the hollows, blinding them with light. As the sun rose higher, the river gleamed like beaten silver.

The Turtle clan lingered, watching the valley fill with heat, color, and light, reluctant to leave their river behind. They sat absolutely still while the snow melted and the sun warmed their arms and faces.

"The Muhekunetuk," Echohawk said softly. "It means 'the water is never still.'"

It felt good to be dressed in his deerskins again. The English clothes had been folded carefully, then rolled into his backpack. Maybe they would come in handy someday.

Echohawk stood up, stretched, and brushed the wet leaves and dirt off his leggings and breechcloth. But the river seemed to draw him to her; it was impossible to turn his back.

Glickihigan was staring at the Muhekunetuk too.

"We have lived on her banks since the first days," he said. "In those first days the Great Turtle rose from the sea so the People, animals, and plants could live on his shell. As long as we are alive, the Great Turtle will stay afloat. If we disappear, he will go under the sea again and the People, animals, and plants will sink with him.

"I wonder: When we turn our backs, will the Great Turtle think we are gone?"

The vast river valley glowed below them: the river, the forests, the towns, the remnants of Algonquin and Iroquois villages now covered in thin new-growth trees. The very air itself spoke to Echohawk of a time and a place irretrievably lost.

"I wonder: When we turn our backs, will everything we see and hear below us sink back into the sea?" Glickihigan asked.

"Father, the Great Turtle can feel us walking on his shell." Bamaineo jumped up and landed hard on his feet. "Jump up and down, Echohawk. So the Great Turtle knows we're still here."

Echohawk smiled. "That is not what our father means, little brother. We will not be here, so—we will not be here."

"I wonder," Glickihigan said softly, "with all our stories and chants about the Muhekunetuk: I wonder, does she have a chant about us?"

He stood up and began to chant:

"Our sister the river
is our favorite aunt;
she is our mother and grandmother.

The Muhekunetuk—
her water is never still.

She feeds her children fish from between her fingers
and shellfish from between her toes.

She unravels basket grass from her skirts
and shakes the waterfowl from her sleeves.

She gives us the smooth stones that adorn
her neck and wrists as a remembrance.

Her water is never still.
Like a good mother, she never stops
loving and feeding her children."

The river was like a shining necklace curving between lush green shoulders. A gust of wind blew toward them, filling their noses with the sharp scent of water.

Glickihigan abruptly turned away. He lifted his backpack and musket out of the melting snow and began climbing. Silently, Echohawk and Bamaineo fell in step behind him.

※　※　※

By noon corn they were hot and thirsty. They stopped to eat at a mountain pass. A waterfall tumbled down from the rocks above and joined a stream as it flowed toward the river. As they stood near the waterfall, tiny droplets covered their sweating faces and hot necks. The air was cold and thick with the droplets. Echohawk felt his lungs cool as he inhaled the drifting spray. The sound of pounding water filled his ears.

They filled their cupped hands from the waterfall and drank and drank of the cold, sweet water.

Bamaineo took out his knife and sliced a little piece of buckskin fringe off his shirt. He placed the finger-sized fringe in the stream. The fringe looked like a tiny canoe floating quickly down a swift river.

"Tell the Muhekunetuk hello," he said. "Tell her we will never forget her."

The stream gurgled over the rocks and down the eastern side of the mountain pass. The tiny canoe was gone.

Noon corn was more strips of smoked venison and more drinks from the waterfall. There was nothing to eat but smoked venison. It would be another moon or more before the black raspberries would be ripe enough to eat. The smoked venison had a bitter, salty taste. Echohawk felt that he could drink water until the sun set and he would still be thirsty.

"Tell about where you lived in *Albany*, Echohawk," Bamaineo called out from the other side of the waterfall. "Tell me what you had to eat and what it felt like to have your hair cut off."

Glickihigan was carefully sprinkling dirt into the depressions left by their footsteps. He looked up sharply.

"Bamaineo," he whispered, "you must be very quiet now. From the western face of the Catskills to where the Susquehanna River breaks in half is Iroquois country. They have not welcomed us into their country, and they will not like it if they know we are here. Do you understand?"

"Why are you telling *me* to be quiet?"

Echohawk and Glickihigan exchanged glances and smiles.

"I am reminding all of us to be quiet, Bamaineo. Tell me, what have you heard about the Iroquois?"

Bamaineo looked at his feet. "They—they eat their prisoners. But first they roast them alive slowly for four or five suns. Sometimes they make a prisoner eat the cooked flesh from his own hands or feet. They kill parents in front of their children. They kill children in front of their parents."

Bamaineo took a deep breath. "Killing a prisoner becomes a festival, a celebration of Iroquois strength. Other villages are invited to watch . . . and eat, too."

Glickihigan said, "How many of these stories about the Iroquois are true?"

Bamaineo looked surprised. "I—I don't know."

"Would you like to meet some Iroquois in their country and ask them how many of these stories are true?"

"No," he whispered.

"Then we must be very quiet. No whispering unless it is absolutely necessary. Think how dangerous the Iroquois are for us. Then think about how dangerous they are for your brother."

"I understand," Bamaineo whispered.

Glickihigan stood up straighter. "As we begin our descent and walk toward the Three Sisters, we will be going deeper into Iroquois country. That means no talking, coughing, sneezing, snoring—"

"No smoking," Echohawk said softly.

"Yes," Glickihigan said grimly, "no smoking. No fires. No hunting. No laughter, no footsteps in the mud. Nothing that will call attention to ourselves. One of us will always have to be awake and on guard. Bamaineo is old enough to stand watch now."

Glickihigan looked severely at his younger son.

"You will not fall asleep while guarding the camp."

"Of course not!"

"If you feel yourself falling asleep, do this, Bamaineo." Glickihigan seized the loose skin between his thumb and forefinger and squeezed hard. "Try this on your own hand."

Bamaineo squeezed.

"Harder."

Bamaineo squeezed so hard his face turned red.

"Harder!"

"Ouch!" he yelped.

Glickihigan nodded. "That is good. When you feel yourself falling asleep, you will squeeze between your thumb and forefinger and not make a sound when it hurts. Then you will stay awake."

"Last winter Bamaineo had nightmares about the Iroquois," Echohawk said softly, "because there were Mohawks in the *school*. He would scream in his sleep."

They both looked at him.

"I do not have nightmares," Bamaineo protested. He stamped his foot. "I can be quiet."

"You are not being quiet now, little brother."

Bamaineo folded his arms in front of him and scowled.

Glickihigan and Echohawk stared hard at him for a long time. Bamaineo scowled harder and glared back at them. Glickihigan nodded. "Good," he mouthed silently.

They began their descent down the mountain pass, stepping on rocks whenever possible to keep from making footprints in the soft earth. If there were no rocks, they tried to walk around the mud. That way their moccasins would pick up no mud to leave footprints when they rejoined the rocks.

Any footprints they did make were carefully washed away with water from nearby streams. Or if there was no water nearby, leaves were placed painstakingly on top of each footprint to hide it, then more leaves scattered randomly on top. It was slow work. Sometimes they didn't go more than two thousand paces before stopping to eat again.

Each night they tried to bathe in a stream or at

least rinse out their clothes. They even soaked their hair to get rid of the human smells of sweat, tanned leather, and smoked meat.

※ ※ ※

Time stretched forward like an endless wampum string.

The background of a string of wampum is from the white whelk shell. The designs on the string are from the rare purple quahog shell. The more purple quahog shell on the string, the more valuable the wampum.

Most of their days were like the white whelk shell. One day was just like another, like pieces of whelk shell strung together. Waking up, morning corn of smoked venison and water, then one foot in front of the other beneath massive stands of pine, oak, walnut, beech, and maple. They headed west, the sun always to their left. Their shadows (when they could see them under the dense canopy of trees) fell to the right at all times.

A stop for noon corn: more smoked venison and water. Then one foot in front of the other again until sundown. More venison and water for evening corn. Then looking for water again for the overnight camp. They washed their clothes and themselves, then stretched out wearily on the forest floor and slept, too tired even to dream. Someone always stood watch for the night.

Then, then, then . . .

Sometimes when the moon was full and the forest was flooded in silver light, Glickihigan motioned to them to keep going. Echohawk sighed and forced himself to put one weary foot in front of the other. They stepped lightly over the dry forest floor. Small animals skittered out of the way, their huge, frightened eyes reflecting the moonlight like pools of shining water.

Echohawk wondered if his voice would go away if he didn't use it soon, the way the English words had. He had already forgotten many of the words, and he'd studied so hard back in school! He was itching to ask Glickihigan—was there an English word for sunlight dappling through the trees? Or for the guiding star in the northern night sky, which they always kept to their right? Was there a word for deer families, sleeping so quietly under the trees that the Turtle clan tripped over a mother and two fawns one muggy, hot, endless day?

Was there a word for being so exhausted that he felt lightheaded, as though his skull hummed with the gnats and mosquitoes that buzzed incessantly around his eyes, nose, and ears? He'd thought he'd been tired at Stillwater, but that was wide-awake compared to now. Even his bones felt tired.

Glickihigan pointed to some moss around the north side of a tree. Echohawk lay down gratefully. As he lay on the moss, too tired to eat noon corn, too tired to drink, Echohawk pretended the moss was his feather bed on Pearl Street.

He curled into a ball, his arms against his face to ward off the gnats and mosquitoes.

Aunt Ruth.

The last time he'd seen her, she was slamming his bedroom door behind her. Her prim, angry face flashed into his mind.

He sighed. *Red Fox was right: Looking into her face was like looking into a mirror. She meant well. She had good cause.*

She must have been terribly lonely, living in that big house with just Mildy to keep her company. If Celia and Sara's family ever claim them, she will be lonesome all over again.

A stick broke behind them. Echohawk and Bamaineo froze as Glickihigan stared silently into the trees. He shook his head as a raccoon waddled away.

Echohawk sighed again. The hardest part was staying alert. It was hard to listen so intently that he could hear the footsteps of every rabbit as it hopped and the voice of every bird as it sang. He even heard the high-pitched whine of insects as they struggled to escape spiders' webs.

It was hard to remember to watch and listen intently, to be on constant alert. The combination of extreme boredom and extreme tension was exhausting. More than once he'd awoken to see Bamaineo fast asleep in the dawntime when he was supposed to be keeping watch. Instead of springing to his knees, testing his senses for danger, Echohawk had rolled over and gone back to sleep too.

Their father never scolded Bamaineo for falling asleep.

Glickihigan knows how tired we are.

Every morning I feel as if I went to sleep just a moment ago. But any shadow might be the Iroquois, any reddish tint among the green leaves and brown tree trunks might be war paint. Any time a branch moves, it might be an arrow, slicing through the air toward our hearts.

Tension and fatigue made the muscles in his neck and shoulders tighten. His scalp clamped down on his skull like a hand squeezing an apple. Echohawk's head throbbed in dull pain all day.

When every day was like the white whelk shell, it was hard to remember the danger. It was also hard not to imagine there were angry Iroquois behind every tree. It was hard to keep from half dozing while one foot stepped in front of the other; it was harder still to keep the panic from prickling the back of his stiff, sore neck.

Tired, hot, thirsty, hungry, footsore, terrified, bored, anxious—

"We are like the deer," he whispered one steamy afternoon while they waited out a shower.

Echohawk couldn't remember the last time he'd said anything.

"Deer live the same lives sun after sun—they

walk down the same paths and drink from the same streams, they eat from the same trees and glades. Their lives never change. But their hearts are filled with fear and panic. We are like the deer."

He looked at his father and brother. "Does that make sense?"

Bamaineo frowned, but Glickihigan nodded.

Then there were days like rare purple quahog shells.

It was late morning as they trod softly through a long glade between giant stands of beech trees. The sun was shimmeringly hot in the glade. Echohawk's throbbing headache was worse, and no matter how much water he drank or how many sassafras twigs he chewed, he could not get the harsh taste of smoked venison out of his mouth.

Glickihigan was walking far ahead. He was out of the glade and among the trees again, his back already in shadow.

Suddenly Bamaineo stopped so abruptly that Echohawk bumped right into him. They fell over. Bamaineo's eyes were bright as he pointed to the bushes around them. "Look, look," he whispered.

Hundreds of black raspberries, glistening purplish red, were still wet from the morning dew.

They rose to their knees and began picking berries. The tangy-sweet flavor of raspberries filled Echohawk's mouth. As his mouth overflowed with juice, he held one hand over his lips so none could escape. He stuffed ten raspberries at once into his mouth, then another ten, then twenty at a time, then thirty at a time.

The sudden rush of sugar in his blood, and the bright sunshine in his eyes, made him sleepy. His eyelids were heavy. The gnats and mosquitoes made a drowsy, humming sound.

Echohawk lay back in the sunshine, and his body seemed to melt into the warm, sweet earth around him. The vivid taste of black raspberries lingered on his tongue. Insects buzzed lazily in the hot glade, lulling him to sleep.

Was there an English word for no more headache?

Footsteps by his shoulder. Echohawk opened one eye.

Glickihigan knelt next to him and shook his shoulder in alarm. Echohawk lifted one hand and opened it. As the black raspberries rolled out of his palm, Glickihigan caught them. He smiled as he popped them into his mouth.

Echohawk sat up and put his lips next to his father's ear.

"Father," he whispered softly, "what is the English word for these berries? We did not learn this word in Mr. Warner's school."

"I do not know this word, Echohawk."

Bamaineo sat down next to them. His cupped hands were full of berries. Sticky juice ran down his chin and neck.

"Can we stay here, Father, for a little while?" he whispered.

"Yes, but lie down so no one can see you."

Bamaineo stretched out in the glade. The rest of his berries rolled out of his hands.

"This has been a good sun. This has been the black-raspberry sun," he whispered before falling fast asleep.

CHAPTER ELEVEN

EYES AND EARS

The Turtle Clan would wait until the middle of the night before silently crossing the creeks and rivers. They were in the middle of the Strawberry Moon when they reached Delaware Creek. Echohawk looked longingly downstream. He watched the creek, lit by starshine, as it drained into the head-waters of the eastern branch of the Susquehanna.

When Echohawk sighed, Glickihigan shook his head as a warning.

"It is much too dangerous to follow Delaware Creek," he said softly. "We have lost this part of our country—it is Iroquois now. They are sure to be swimming, fishing, or living next to her riverbanks. We will build a raft when it is safe. Soon we will be floating down our part of the Susquehanna."

Head down, half asleep, Bamaineo bumped into Echohawk's back.

"Did you hear that, little brother? A raft will be easier than walking."

Bamaineo shrugged his shoulders. "When can we rest again?" he asked.

❈ ❈ ❈

At the end of the Strawberry Moon, Bamaineo's toes burst through his moccasins. It was the only pair he had.

His feet were growing so fast that his toes had pushed against the insides, stretching the already thin leather to the breaking point. The thinning leather was further worn down on the outside, because Bamaineo was so weary that he dragged his feet at every step and stumbled over every rock.

"Do your feet hurt?" Glickihigan whispered when Bamaineo wriggled his bare toes. "Can you walk?"

Bamaineo just shrugged his shoulders.

"Soon we will be crossing the Unadilla River, and then the Chenango. That will be something different, not just the same thing sun after sun," Echohawk whispered.

Bamaineo shrugged again.

Ever since the black-raspberry sun, Bamaineo had become quieter and quieter. But it was not a good sort of quiet. It was as though the farther they walked from home, the more his spirit withdrew inside him, like a turtle pulling into its shell.

He brought up the rear, his gaze always fastened on his feet. Whenever they sat down to rest or eat, Bamaineo sat down first and stood up last. As they rested, sometimes he just stared into space and chewed slowly, whether he had any food in his mouth or not.

Bamaineo's eyes were dull and rimmed with red. His shoulders and jaw slumped. There were deep hollows above his cheekbones. It was becoming more and more difficult to wake him for morning corn.

It was hot and still. Echohawk missed the fresh mountain air and the cool breezes blowing through the Catskills. A constant cloud of gnats buzzed around his face. They stuck in his eyes and even up his nose if he inhaled too hard. After a swarm of buzzing, bitter-tasting bugs had flown into his mouth, he'd learned to keep his lips clamped shut.

The Turtle clan took to sleeping during the worst heat of the day, and that helped a little. To keep the insects and the heat at bay, the two lucky enough to sleep draped Echohawk's fine linen shirt over their faces as they napped.

It was another hot, sleepy afternoon as Echohawk kept watch while his father and brother slept under the linen shirt.

"How can the weather be so muggy if we've had no rain?" he muttered to himself.

The creek bed in front of him was almost dry.

What little water was left looked more like a thin trail of blood winding along the forest floor than a stream. Tiny fish flipped and flopped in alarm, gasping for breath in the cracking mud.

At least my English clothes have come in handy. Aunt Ruth was so proud of that shirt. All the way from Ireland, wherever that is. The same place the soldiers sent Smoke Eyes. I wonder if he's wearing a shirt like this one now.

Echohawk wearily brushed the gnats away from his face. He cupped his hands over his nose and took deep, bugless breaths to try to ease his jittery nerves and racing heart.

Someone has been following us. There, I have put my terror into words.

There was no place he could point to exactly. He couldn't say, "It was by that larch tree that I knew," or "Next to that dried-up swamp is where I realized the truth."

Rather, the terror sprang from something he *was*. The awful dread racing through his mind came from years and years of living by his wits in the forest. His intuition made his heart sink. His apprehension made his nightmares as vivid as the black raspberries. He was as jumpy as a cricket, and his feet itched to run, run, run!

Someone has been following us.

Bamaineo can hardly walk, much less run. Glick-ihigan grows more weary every day. I can't tell them. Their fear would only make this journey worse.

It was a curious feeling, keeping silent because he didn't want his father and brother to be afraid. It felt as though he were carrying them on his shoulders as he staggered through the forest.

Maybe we'll be in our own territory before they catch us.

※ ※ ※

At evening corn the heat still kept an iron grip on the day. As they sat under a huge oak and Glickihigan passed around slices of the same old venison, Bamaineo watched his toes wriggling slowly. They stuck out completely from what was left of his moccasins. He wasn't hungry. Again.

After they had eaten, Glickihigan drew Echohawk aside. "Walk behind your brother at all times," he whispered. "Do not let him fall behind. That way, if he falls and does not have the strength to get up again, we won't leave him by mistake."

All that evening, every time Bamaineo's toes caught on a tree root or his instep landed on a sharp rock, he winced or yelped in pain. By the time their shadows were softening against the rocks and tree trunks, Bamaineo was whimpering constantly.

The moccasins' loose soles made a flapping sound with every step. The evening breeze picked up the sound as though it were a feather and carried it throughout the silent forest.

Flap, flap, flappity-flap . . .

The noise grated on Echohawk's nerves. His headache came back, throbbing worse than ever. His neck and shoulders felt as stiff as wood.

Someone is following us.

Closely. There was something in the air, the faint smell of campfire, of burning tobacco; once he thought he'd heard the low murmuring of voices carried by the wind.

What he'd thought was gurgling water in the distance—a perfect place to stay tonight!—now he was certain was laughter bouncing off the tree trunks.

"Bamaineo, please. Stop making so much noise with your feet," he whispered softly. "Please."

Bamaineo stumbled on.

Flap, flap, flappity-flap . . .

When they stopped to rest next to a dry creek bed, Bamaineo's feet were bleeding onto the light-gray stones.

Glickihigan shook his head and pointed at the path behind them. On the rocks were bloody-red footprints, unmistakably human.

Bamaineo's eyes were as big as an owl's.

"The Iroquois will think a bear," he whispered.

"They will think a boy or a girl or a young woman," Glickihigan whispered fiercely. "Someone who would not be traveling alone. And they will know this boy, or girl, or young woman is injured and cannot run from them."

"It will rain. The blood will wash away."

"Not before they see the footprints, Bamaineo," Echohawk whispered. His eyes were angry yellow-brown slits. "It has not rained for a long time. Look."

He pointed at the branches of a hemlock, the tips of the leaves brown and withered.

"And look." He pointed at the dirt around them. Tiny sassafras and dogwood trees drooped, their yellowing leaves touching the cracks in the dry earth.

"No rain, little brother. And no stream nearby to wash away the bloody trail you have left."

Bamaineo sat down against a tree trunk and thrust his feet forward. He looked up at the angry faces glaring down at him.

"My feet hurt," he said tearfully. "They are bleeding. I can't walk anymore. We have been so careful; no one is on our trail."

"What are you thinking?" Glickihigan snapped. "Stay here, and wait for the Iroquois to follow the trail you have left for them? We must walk faster now. Faster."

Bamaineo took off his moccasins and made a show of wringing them out. Bloody sweat splattered onto the sassafras plants, glowing bright red against the greenish-yellow leaves.

Echohawk glared at his brother while kicking powder-dry earth onto the bloodied plants.

"I can't walk anymore," Bamaineo said stubbornly. "No one is following us."

Echohawk put his foot on his brother's knee. When he spoke, he thought of a snake biting into the softest part of its victim.

"Little brother, soon we will all be dead because of you."

Bamaineo gasped. Even Glickihigan looked surprised.

Bamaineo's chin started to tremble. "I don't care anymore," he wailed. "I want to go home. I want to go home, to our camp by the waterfall."

"Bamaineo, you must be quiet—" Glickihigan began.

"My feet are hurt and bleeding, and I'm thirsty and I'm hungry and I want to go home and I WANT MY MOTHER!" Bamaineo screamed.

Echohawk and Glickihigan stared at him, stunned. The word "mother" echoed down the creek bed and over the treetops. The wind carried Bamaineo's cry in all directions.

"I WANT MY—"

Glickihigan sprang at him, covering Bamaineo's mouth with his hand. "Bamaineo, you will make no more noise. None. You have promised us. No talking until we reach the Susquehanna and we are in our own country again."

Tears spilled out of Bamaineo's eyes and onto his cheeks. They ran down the back of his father's hand.

"Bamaineo, we will rest. Soon. Your brother is right—it has not rained. The ground is so dry, we do not have to worry about muddy footprints. We no longer have to walk on the rocks. The dry earth will be softer for your feet. Will you be quiet?"

Glickihigan took his hand away.

"I WANT MY MOTHER!"

Glickihigan capped Bamaineo's mouth again. "Bamaineo, you will stop. Stop."

Echohawk knelt next to them. "He cried a lot when you were away last winter," he whispered. "He will stop when he is tired."

"He is tired now. That is why he is crying."

Glickihigan pressed his son's face into the hollow of his shoulder. He rocked him back and forth. Bamaineo's sobs were muffled by the soft deerskin shirt.

"Shh . . . shh . . . You must be quiet. Shh . . . Listen, Bamaineo, do you remember? Your mother used to call you Honeybee. I can hear Windsong now, calling you home for evening corn: 'Honeybee, Honeybee.' Do you remember that?"

Echohawk drew his breath in sharply. Eighteen moons had passed since his mother's death. No one was supposed to say her name. No one ever talked about the dead. Ever.

"She used to call me Bear Cub," Echohawk whispered. "Do you remember, Bamaineo? She— Windsong used to call us Bear Cub and Honeybee."

"Why did she call you Honeybee? Do you remember?" Glickihigan asked Bamaineo.

"Because I like . . . honey . . . so much," Bamaineo sobbed.

"And because you stick to your brother, as though

he were a bear cub with honey smeared on his fur."

Bamaineo cried for a long time, his face pressed tightly against his father's shirt, while Glickihigan whispered to him.

"Shh . . . Bamaineo. It is all right. I am sorry. I forget you are only eight winters. I forget you must take two steps for every one of ours. I forget you would rather be playing and swimming in our river. I forget you are a little boy with sore feet.

"Shh . . . Honeybee. I will kill two rabbits, and we will wrap your sore feet in their warm fur. Will soft fur against your sore feet make them feel better?"

Bamaineo's sobs spaced further and further apart. He wrapped his arms around his father's neck.

"What can I do?" Glickihigan whispered in his ear. "What can I say to make you stop crying?"

"Call me Honeybee again."

Chapter Twelve

THE DARK JOY

It was already dusk. Glickihigan tucked his bow and arrows under his arm and motioned for them not to make a sound.

"Father," Echohawk whispered. "The Iroquois—"

His father drew him aside.

"Yes. They are following us."

"You know this?" Echohawk said, surprised. "So do I."

"I didn't want to worry you," Glickihigan replied.

"I didn't want to worry *you*."

Glickihigan shook his head. "I'm sorry, Echohawk. Sometimes I forget you're a man. We should have been working together, and I was trying to protect you as though you were still a boy."

He squeezed Echohawk's shoulders. "You *are* a man. I am so proud of you. We must get into

Delaware country again as fast as possible. Hide under this pine. Do you see how the branches sweep the ground? They won't see you if you stay quiet."

"But—"

Glickihigan turned away.

Echohawk found a sweet gum tree and peeled the gummy sap off the bark. As he chewed it, the sweet-tart sap made his mouth water. He spat the liquefied sap out in his hands and rubbed Bamaineo's feet with it. But his brother's feet were dirty, and there was no water to wash them with before rubbing the sap onto the broken skin.

"Tomorrow, little brother," he whispered. "Tomorrow we will wash your feet, then find more sap. Your feet will heal faster."

The sweet gum was already beginning to work. As it hardened again on the raw, bloody skin, Bamaineo's feet stopped bleeding. The gnats and black flies left his feet alone.

"My feet sting now," Bamaineo complained. His eyes filled with tears. "Cold water would feel so good."

"We don't have cold water, any water. Don't start crying again. We will wait for Glickihigan under that pine."

They ducked under the pine tree, the thick, sweeping branches hiding them completely. Echohawk set the muskets against the tree trunk and hung the backpacks deep within the pine boughs.

They gnawed on slices of smoked venison. The meat was as dry as leather, and it stuck in Echohawk's throat.

"We need water to wash the venison down, Echohawk."

"There is no water, little brother. Shh."

"When will our father come back?"

"I don't know. He is so tired, and you have sent him looking for rabbits," Echohawk scolded.

"But he offered to look for rabbits."

"You could have told him no. You haven't noticed how he pants for air all the time? How slowly he walks?"

"No."

"Sometimes when it is his turn to stand watch, I can't wake him up. He sleeps like the dead."

Bamaineo thought for a moment.

"He can walk to the Three Sisters, can't he, Echohawk?"

"He thinks he can, and that is what matters. Please be quiet, little brother. I need to listen."

"Listen to what?"

"To everything."

The birds had gone to sleep. The shrilling tree frogs had not yet awakened. It was quiet except for the rush of wind in the trees and the constant humming of insects.

Tomorrow marked the beginning of the Moon of Longest Days, when the sun stayed in the sky long after everyone grew sleepy and rose again long before anyone felt like waking up. Usually this was

Echohawk's favorite moon. There was plenty of sunlight for hunting, for running races, for swimming in the river, for long feasts of fresh summer food in the purple twilight.

During the Moon of Longest Days the earth tilted herself toward the warming sun, like a sleeping baby turning her face toward the heat of a starfire.

Glickihigan is counting on the Moon of Longest Days for fast walking, Echohawk thought. His brother lay sound asleep next to him, the stiffening sap from the sweet gum filling the air with its sharp scent.

But Bamaineo can't walk.

And the sunlight is our enemy.

Echohawk rested his head against the tree trunk. He moved his head slowly from side to side, pressing his cheeks into the rough bark. As he moved his head, the muscles in his shoulders and neck creaked and popped like old leather. His head throbbed like a drum. The headache made his stomach queasy.

He could not rid himself of a growing sense of catastrophe, of bloody horror lurking behind that tree or hiding behind that rock. So many things had gone wrong—Glickihigan worn out, his capture, the bloody footprints, the sore feet, Bamaineo screaming in the middle of the silence, saying his mother's name out loud, no water to drink or wash with, their father going off and leaving them in the middle of Iroquois country.

It is too quiet. We have already been tracked and found. Perhaps they are watching this tree even now.

It had been six winters ago when Makwa of the Bear clan had marched a French trapper into their camp by the waterfall. The prisoner had been in their country, trapping animals that belonged to them.

He had been an enemy and had deserved to die.

He had been tied up, scalped, then burned to death. But it had taken three long suns for the Frenchman to die.

While the Frenchman slowly died, his hands and feet were crushed with war clubs, severed, then burned to cinders in the fire. Makwa bound the Frenchman's arms and legs tighter, so he wouldn't bleed to death and die too quickly.

That first horrible night the Frenchman sobbed and screamed till sunrise. Echohawk lay on his sleeping platform and stared up at the wigwam ceiling, listening and thinking. *What was he doing in our country in the first place? Didn't he know he was not supposed to be here? Don't Frenchmen know what a disgrace it is, crying like a baby in front of other men?*

At sunrise the clans stepped bleary-eyed out of the wigwams. No one else had been able to sleep either, so after that Makwa gagged the trapper at night.

During each sun, as they danced around the

screaming, smoldering prisoner, Echohawk felt a sort of dark joy in his heart. He could see that same joy in all their faces.

By midmorning on the third sun, the Frenchman stopped screaming. His face was encircled by fire. At his moment of death the Frenchman stared right at Echohawk, and it seemed to Echohawk that the Frenchman was noticing his white skin and yellow-brown eyes for the first time.

He was an enemy and deserved to die.

But for a long time afterward no one in the Turtle clan could look another straight in the eye. Shamefaced, Echohawk spent time by himself in the forest. Once he saw his father sitting alone against a tree trunk, staring into space. Instead of joining him, Echohawk turned away.

Bamaineo had been only two winters and had suffered from nightmares until the season changed. Their mother had served their favorite foods and told them stories about gentle spirits helping those with gentle hearts.

We are as bad as the Iroquois, Echohawk thought suddenly. *We are so terrified of the Iroquois because when we hear stories about them, we know we are really hearing stories about ourselves.*

Bamaineo stirred in his sleep. "What are you listening for, Echohawk?"

"Shh . . . Everything. Go back to sleep."

"Are you listening for our father?"

"Yes, little brother. Go to sleep."

"Good night."

It was full dark and the shrilling of the tree frogs filled his ears. Echohawk was sure Bamaineo was sleeping.

"Echohawk?"

"Shhh."

"Do you remember when you saw my spirit-brother at the last Freezing Moon?"

"How could I forget? I saw the bamain, the great male elk, standing in deep snow. By now his antlers are bigger than you."

"You told him we would be going back to our camp by the waterfall. Perhaps he is waiting for me along the banks of the Muhekunetuk."

"Little brother, your spirit-helper always knows where you are. And when you need his help, he will be there to help you."

"But you said he was my spirit-brother," Bamaineo persisted, "not my spirit-helper. Which one is he?"

"Maybe he is both."

Bamaineo sat up. "How can he be both—"

"Little brother," Echohawk said impatiently, "I can't tell you which one he is. But someday *you* will know; the answer will enter your heart. Did our father ever tell you about his Vision Quest?"

"Tell me the story once more, Echohawk," Bamaineo said as he lay down again.

"He saw his spirit-helper, a wolf mother, fierce, and guarding her cubs. One of those cubs was a fox."

"And?"

"*I* was the fox. He'd had his Vision Quest at thirteen winters, just like everyone else. But he did not understand what it meant for another thirty winters! When he found me, he knew; the answer had entered his heart. The same thing will happen to you. You will know if that bamain is your spirit-helper or spirit-brother. Or both. Go to sleep, Bamaineo."

"Tell me about your Vision Quest, Echohawk."

"I can't tell you what I don't understand."

But he did understand his Vision Quest. He'd seen a pack of wolves, then a hawk flying alone. What else could that mean but that he'd be alone someday?

Bamaineo whined, "I'm tired of venison all the time. I wish we had more black raspberries."

"Shh . . . There will be plenty to eat at the Three Sisters. Go to sleep, Bamaineo. Soon we will be in Delaware country again. We will build a raft and float down the Susquehanna. Long, lazy days with plenty of time to rest.

"And when we reach the Three Sisters, there will be more food than we can eat, more new friends than we can name.

"As the years pass, we will be great sachems, Bamaineo. We are Turtle clan, and our children and grandchildren will be Turtle clan too. We will have a good, peaceful life."

Bamaineo said, "Blueberries will ripen next."

"Shhh. Not another word."

Echohawk meant to stand watch but drifted off

to sleep instead. While he slept, he dreamed of a ring of fire and the Frenchman's blistering red face in the center, staring into his own.

CHAPTER THIRTEEN

THE WOLF AND THE HAWK

The next dream was much better.

He was in his wife's wigwam along the Oyosipi—the Ohio River. At evening corn the wigwam was crowded with laughing children, fine girls and strong boys. It gave him much pleasure to look into the faces of his children. It was like looking into a mirror—they all had his yellow-brown eyes, his broad forehead and nose.

The cooking pot bubbled with venison, wild turkey, duck, and rabbit. He was a sachem, the best hunter among the clans, and worked hard to teach his sons everything he knew. Never had there been a hunting trip when he and his sons came back empty-handed.

Bamaineo was married to his wife's sister. That

meant they didn't have to live in separate villages. Their two families were always together, as close as brothers and sisters.

As they ate, their grandfather, who lived in warm comfort on a buffalo robe close to the starfire, told them stories of hunting in the far north, in the Canadas, where it was much colder than along the banks of the Oyosipi.

It was night, and the wigwam was full of sleeping children.

Bamaineo's youngest son sat up. *"Help,"* he said. *"Echohawk, help."*

"What is wrong?" he asked.

"Echohawk! Echohawk! Help!"

Echohawk sat up. Shrill, urgent screaming filled his ears.

He scrambled out from under the tree. It was late morning, by the sun's slant. How could he have slept so long? Where was Bamaineo? Where was Glickihigan?

The screaming rushed toward him, louder and louder. It was Bamaineo, racing toward him with a thundercloud of bees buzzing around his ears.

"I followed a bee line to a honey tree," he screamed. "I wanted honey! Make them stop stinging me. Make them stop! Stop!"

Echohawk peeled a branch off another pine tree and beat the air around his brother's head with it. The cloud of bees reared up like a living thing. Bees swirled around their heads in angry confusion.

Then one bee flew away, and the black cloud whirled away to follow.

Bamaineo howled as his face began to bloat up like a pumpkin. His eyes were swollen almost shut. Tears squeezed out from between his eyelids like sap oozing out of a spruce gum tree.

"I wanted some honey!" he screamed. "Make it stop hurting!"

"Be quiet!" Echohawk shouted. "We will find some mud to coat your face. You will feel better."

Echohawk led his brother to a creek bed they'd crossed the evening before. Bamaineo sat down on the creek bed and howled. His toes and the soles of his feet were bleeding again.

"You must be quiet," Echohawk said. "They will hear you. Be quiet, little brother."

"I can't walk! I can't see!" Bamaineo screamed.

"You can see, Bamaineo," Echohawk said in a soothing voice. "Lift your face to the sun and look down your nose. There, you can see me, right?"

Bamaineo sobbed, "Make it stop hurting!"

Echohawk reached into the middle of the drying creek bed for some mud. He gently dabbed mud on the bee stings that covered Bamaineo's face, arms, and legs.

"Do you feel better?"

"No!"

"Stop crying, Bamaineo. You'll wash away the mud.

"We'll wait under the pine tree for Glickihigan. He should be here soon. He'll have soft rabbit skins for you, remember? He promised. Rabbit skins for your feet and now mud for your face."

Echohawk took his brother's hands. Walking backward, he guided Bamaineo toward the pine tree, speaking softly to him all the time about the new camp at the Three Sisters.

"It will be just as good as the camp by the waterfall but better, little brother," Echohawk murmured. "Better because there are no English at the Three Sisters. Do you see our pine behind me? You look for me, Bamaineo. Your eyes will be our eyes."

Bamaineo pried one of his eyes open with his fingers and screamed again.

The Mohawks were waiting for them at the pine tree.

❈ ❈ ❈

The brothers' wrists were tied behind them with grapevines. Their ankles were also tied, but loosely, so they could walk but not run.

Once their wrists and ankles were tied securely, one of the Mohawks reached into his waist pouch. He held his hand in front of Echohawk's nose and slowly opened it. On the palm was one perfectly ripened black raspberry.

"What are they doing, Echohawk?" Bamaineo tilted his chin up as far as it would go and looked down his nose at the Mohawks. "I can't see them."

"They have been following us since we ate the

black raspberries," Echohawk said sadly. "Since your black-raspberry sun."

"If they have found us, they have found our father, too," Bamaineo whispered.

"Don't say anything about him—"

The other Mohawk sprang at him like a panther, striking Echohawk so hard that he fell backward.

His headache exploded against the inside of his skull in a burst of sharp, jagged light. His stomach lurched, and he threw up yellow liquid, sour and bitter on his tongue. A wave of fever washed over him as he coughed; his headache throbbed harder.

The Mohawk grabbed Echohawk by the hair and dragged him to his feet. As he shouted, Echohawk kept his eyes downcast. Abruptly the Mohawk stopped shouting. He grasped Echohawk's chin and held his face up to the sunshine. The Mohawk stared hard into Echohawk's eyes, then shouted to his friend.

The second Mohawk sliced Echohawk's deerskin shirt with a knife. They stared open-mouthed at his white skin and the turtle tattoos on his chest that marked him as a Turtle clan warrior.

"You're white," the first Mohawk said in English.

"You're English!" the other one shouted.

They turned their attention toward Bamaineo. They held his face up to the sun too. The bee stings, his sore and bleeding feet, his hunger and thirst, his exhaustion, his missing father, and the Mohawks were all too much for Bamaineo. He was bawling like a baby.

"Delaware," Echohawk said softly. "Mohican."

The Mohawks laughed and pushed them forward. At the first step Bamaineo fell down. His crying became shrill, and instead of rising to his feet, he curled into a ball.

Echohawk pretended to fall down next to him.

"Get up, little brother," he whispered in his brother's ear. "If you don't get up, they'll kill you. Stand up with me."

Bamaineo stumbled to his feet as Echohawk held his arm. Bamaineo took a few steps. His feet left bloody footprints in the pine needles.

"I can't see!" Bamaineo screamed. "I can't walk!"

"Little brother, be strong!"

The Mohawks pointed at Bamaineo and argued with each other. One pulled his tomahawk from his belt.

"No!" Echohawk shouted in English. "No! I'll carry him!"

The other threw Bamaineo over his shoulder as though he were a felled deer.

"White boy," the Mohawk who carried Bamaineo said. He gestured with his arm to start walking.

Echohawk stepped forward, careful not to look at the pine tree. Their muskets and gear were still hidden under the branches.

Where have I seen these Mohawks before? he thought. *The one short, the other tall—I have seen them somewhere.*

They marched to the north-northwest. Echohawk had to struggle to keep up.

The Iroquois—that means "the terrifying men." The

Mohawk, the Oneida, the Onondaga, the Seneca, the Cayuga, and the Tuscarora. *The terrifying men—the Iroquois.*

We've been captured by the Iroquois.

It was a hot morning, but his blood raced through him freezing cold. His entire body was trembling.

Bamaineo said, "Killing a prisoner becomes a festival, a celebration of Iroquois strength."

The Frenchman—

As his heart pounded, his headache throbbed against his skull. His vision blackened around the edges. Echohawk stopped to rub his eyes. The Mohawk walking behind him shoved him so hard that he fell again.

But why have we been caught by Mohawks? Echohawk thought, scrambling to his feet. *We left their territory at the Dogwood Moon. We must be in Oneida land by now, or maybe Onondaga, and we're heading northwest, even farther away from Mohawk land. It makes no sense.*

Where is Glickihigan?

The Iroquois live in longhouses, some as long as one hundred eighty paces. Four or five families all live in the same one. It will be hard to escape from such a longhouse.

Mohawk, Oneida, Onondaga, Cayuga, Seneca, Tuscarora . . . reciting the nation names again and again crowded the terror out of his mind. Mohawk, Oneida, Onondaga, Cayuga, Seneca, Tuscarora . . .

We've been captured by Iroquois—Iroquois!

I'm so hungry and thirsty. Will I ever eat again? Will I ever taste cold, sweet water again?

They stopped by a muddy stream that evening. Echohawk and Bamaineo lay on their stomachs and slurped at the muddy water. Bamaineo stuck his entire face in the mud to relieve his bee stings.

The Mohawks untied their hands for the night. One Mohawk slept while the other stood watch. Echohawk lay down and pretended to sleep. But his mind was racing as fast as his heart.

Where is Glickihigan? He should have returned last night. He's either dead or captured too.

They wouldn't kill boys, would they? If I was adopted by the Delaware, perhaps we could be adopted by the Iroquois. Stranger things have happened. But Bamaineo looks terrible, his face all swollen and his feet a bloody pulp. Who would want us?

"If you pretend to be happy, they will stop watching you."

Glickihigan's voice rang in his ears as though his father were lying down next to him.

Echohawk closed his eyes and saw Glickihigan's calm face, smiling and nodding to him.

Of course! When they stop watching us, we can escape and look for him. I need to sleep. I need to be ready for anything tomorrow.

Echohawk took deep breaths and concentrated all his panic into calmness. His heart and mind stopped racing, his muscles stopped twitching. He drifted off to sleep.

✻ ✻ ✻

The Mohawks did not stop watching them. If one slept or looked for water or food, the other didn't take his eyes off the prisoners for one moment.

It was two suns later, at sundown, when the prisoners sat in front of a family's cookfire in the center of a longhouse. They had been untied and their grapevine bands thrown into the fire so they could watch them burning. They were given plenty of hot water to wash with. An older woman gave them bowlful after bowlful of cool water to drink.

When they'd had their fill of water, she dabbed mud on Bamaineo's bee stings. Echohawk looked at his own forearms in surprise. They were swollen with bee stings and he hadn't even noticed, so much had happened since the bee attack.

The old woman bathed Bamaineo's feet, then applied a soothing paste of water mixed with powdered willow bark. She wrapped his feet with strips of the softest deerskin. New moccasins lay waiting by the fire.

Echohawk looked longingly at the pieces of willow bark stuck in her open medicine pouch. *If I could chew just a little, my headache will go away. My forearms are starting to hurt too.*

The old woman bade them sit closer to the fire. She served them steaming bowls of delicious rabbit stew with wild carrots and onions. The Mohawks had given them a few strips of leathery venison to eat on the march. Echohawk and Bamaineo were starving; she filled their bowls again and again.

"Why is she being so nice to us?" Bamaineo whispered. "Where is our father?"

"Nice to you, you mean. Ask her if I can have some willow bark to chew. My headache is back, worse than ever."

Bamaineo motioned to his brother and held his head in his hands. The older woman tossed Echohawk a piece of willow bark without even looking at him. She had eyes only for Bamaineo.

A faint glimmer of hope warmed Echohawk's heart. *She wants my brother.*

Echohawk chewed the bitter-tasting bark and searched all the faces in front of them. It was hard to see through the dark, smoky air. A crowd of sullen faces stared back at him. None of them was Glickihigan.

After they'd finished eating, the two Mohawks who'd captured the brothers marched them out into the camp. A throng of people followed. Echohawk looked around him, eager to plan an escape. The camp was made up of five longhouses and a common building for dried stored food. The camp lay next to a long, narrow lake.

Sparkling water shimmered behind the longhouses and trees. Canoes and fishing nets lay onshore.

They marched into the center of the camp and into the longest of the longhouses.

They passed seven cookfires as they went down a

long hallway. All the clans followed them to the very end of the longhouse.

Glickihigan was sitting by the fire, with four guards surrounding him.

"Father!" the brothers shouted at once.

"I have seen her," he whispered softly as Echohawk and Bamaineo rushed into his arms. "My spirit-helper. I've told you about her, Echohawk. She is here."

"Yes. A mother wolf, fierce, guarding her cubs. One of them was a fox."

"An Onondaga hunting party found me as I was skinning rabbits. My spirit-helper loped beside us as they brought me here. She was hiding behind the trees, looking at me at every step. She is here. How curious that you and your brother are here too."

"This is an Onondaga camp? They have been kind to us," Echohawk whispered in his ear. "They have fed us, they gave us hot water to wash with, and an old woman has treated Bamaineo's feet and his bee stings. She gave me willow bark for my headache. It is going away."

"Bee stings? Headache?"

"They have been kind to you?" Echohawk asked.

His father shook his head.

"I know where our muskets are hidden," Echohawk continued. "When we escape, we can retrieve them."

Glickihigan said nothing and stared at the roaring fire.

The Mohawks came forward.

One of them began to speak. "Welcome, Mohicans and our English guest. I have traded on your river and I know some of your language. My name is Avousent. That means 'Squirrel.'"

Of course, Echohawk thought. *I saw these Mohawk traders in front of the Indian House, in Albany! They've been tracking us since then. We never had a chance.*

Avousent pointed to the old woman who'd taken such good care of Bamaineo. "Yellow Eel of the Snake clan lost her son last winter. He was checking his fishing lines in the ice holes down the lake when the Susquehannans took him. The Susquehannans are our Delaware neighbors to the south."

Avousent glared at the Turtle clan.

"Those thieves have their own river, but they come up here to steal our fish and our children."

"Yellow Eel's son is safe," Glickihigan said softly. "Someone who lost a son has adopted Yellow Eel's son."

Maybe Yellow Eel will want me too, Echohawk thought.

Avousent continued, "But now Yellow Eel has no son. She will take your younger son into the Snake clan to heal her heart."

Yellow Eel smiled at Bamaineo and said something.

Avousent translated, "Yellow Eel says, 'You will have many sisters in the Snake clan, and you will have the bride her son was meant to have.'"

"No," Bamaineo whispered. "No."

"Bamaineo," Glickihigan said softly, "you have a chance to survive, and you will take that chance."

"I want to stay with you."

"English!" Avousent shouted. "I have just come from *Albany*, and I have learned something of great interest. *Patroon* Henrick Van Rensselaer will give ten pieces of gold for any white captive among the nations. I will take you back to *Albany* and sell you there."

The ransom! All this way for nothing.

"I prefer to be a slave," Echohawk said softly. "I work hard. I can be with my brother, and my father, too," he said hopefully.

Avousent laughed. "Ten pieces of gold will trade for two muskets. You are worth more to us as muskets than as a slave. One musket for the Onondaga, and one musket for us."

"Echohawk," Glickihigan said softly.

"No, don't say it."

"You have a chance to survive, and you will take that chance. Ask *Patroon* Henrick Van Rensselaer to give you back to your aunt."

"No, no—"

"You have praised her *horse*. Think how good it will be to see her *horse* again. And there is *Latin and Greek*." Glickihigan smiled at him. "In the future, if you see your brother in the woods, know that he is not your enemy."

"But I want to be with you. We want to be with you."

"No, you don't. Not yet." Glickihigan had a faraway look in his eyes. "I will see your mother soon. I will tell her how much her children miss her."

Avousent shouted, "We don't want you. We don't

want a slave with ugly pale skin and yellow eyes like a forest demon's."

He shouted to the Onondagas, and they all nodded their heads and shouted back.

"I can see. We can escape now," Bamaineo cried. He looked out from under eyelids that were still swollen.

"The English will never live in Iroquois country," Avousent shouted. "You Delaware have become weak as women. You no longer even fight the English."

Avousent shouted to the Onondagas, and they roared in approval. They formed a circle around the prisoners, their eyes lit up in excitement.

The dark joy.

"Honeybee," Glickihigan said gently, "you must not look at me. Don't look. Remember the good times. Remember our camp by the waterfall. Promise me, both of you. Promise you will not look.

"I have ten buckeyes in my waist pouch. When I eat five, my limbs will be numb. When I eat another three, my brain will be numb. And when I eat the last two, I will die before these Iroquois have a chance to kill me."

"I am Turtle! I will not be Snake!" Bamaineo shouted at Avousent. "You can't make me!"

"You will be quiet." Avousent grasped Bamaineo's swollen lower lip and twisted it.

Bamaineo screamed in pain.

Yellow Eel rushed out of the crowd of Onondagas and tackled Avousent to the ground. She knelt on his back and grabbed his braids like the reins of a horse's bridle. Yellow Eel opened her wrinkled lips and howled. The Onondagas began to argue among themselves. Some tried to pull Yellow Eel away, others tried to keep her in place.

A low growl filled the dark, smoky air. Glickihigan sat up straight, cocked his head, and listened.

"She is coming," Glickihigan said. "Do you hear her?"

The growl grew louder and angrier. Yellow Eel stopped screaming. The Onondagas stopped arguing. Echohawk felt the growl vibrate through his bones.

"She is here," Glickihigan said, "my spirit-helper. She has come for us."

The Onondagas stood rooted to the floor of the longhouse in terror. The growl filled the air, louder than thunder, louder than the pounding spray of a waterfall.

Echohawk looked around wildly.

They are no longer watching us! An escape—

Just a few paces away from the family cookfire was the end of the longhouse. Just as in his mother's wigwam, and in Redbird's too, old pine needles were piled up between the floor and the wall.

Brown pine needles . . . the fire . . .

Above the deep growling the harsh cries of a hawk scattered frightened Onondagas in all directions.

Echohawk reached into the edge of the cookfire and grabbed hold of a piece of burning kindling by the cool end. He pressed the fiery end against the dried pine needles. They burst into a long line of flames. The bottom of the longhouse wall caught fire.

With both hands Echohawk took hold of a burning log by the cool end and swung it against the burning longhouse wall with all his strength. The old wood shattered open.

"Run!" Glickihigan shouted.

The Turtle clan tumbled out of the longhouse.

A cloud raced in front of the full Moon of Longest Days.

It was light enough to see, yet dark enough to hide.

The Turtle clan ran through the woods, running from tree to tree, Echohawk leading the way. In front of him was the hawk, flying straight as an arrow southward, toward the Susquehanna.

Finally they stopped to catch their breath and listen.

No Onondagas or Mohawks had dared to follow them.

"I can see!" Bamaineo exclaimed. "I saw my bamain, my elk! Did you see him, Echohawk? He did follow me from the Muhekunetuk after all."

"I was watching my hawk, little brother," Echohawk said.

They turned to look at their father.

"My spirit-helper has been following us," Glickihigan said, his voice filled with awe. "She's been telling me, 'Have courage, my brother, be strong. Your journey is almost over.'"

The cloud blew away from the moon, flooding the forest with silvery light. They heard the weight of great animals crashing through the underbrush and the beat of strong, steady wings.

CHAPTER FOURTEEN
WHEN TIME RESTS

In late summer, during the Moon of Ripe Berries, there is always plenty to eat.

In this Moon of Ripe Berries the berry bushes on the Susquehanna riverbanks were so loaded with fruit that the branches bowed down toward the flowing water. Blackberries, huckleberries, elderberries, blueberries, gooseberries, chokecherries—there was more fruit than the Turtle clan could eat. The bright purple and red juices ran from the bursting berries, staining their raft.

After retrieving their backpacks and muskets, the Turtle clan had headed straight south, toward the Susquehanna.

They were now well out of Iroquois country. Anyone the Turtle clan met along the way would be

Delaware. Echohawk, Glickihigan, and Bamaineo would be welcome at any camp along the waterway.

They had made the raft from tall, straight pine saplings stripped of their branches. Glickihigan and Bamaineo were strong enough to slice their deerskin shirts into thin strips and soak the thongs in the river. Echohawk lashed the logs together. As the thongs dried, they shrank, making the raft secure and watertight.

The Turtle clan floated slowly down the midstream. There was nothing to do during these lazy days except check the nets and decide which berries to eat when they stopped for evening corn.

One would navigate the wide, gentle river while the other two dozed in the hot sunshine.

Glickihigan had woven the fishing nets of grapevines and lashed them to the back of the raft. At sunset there were plump fish in the nets to be roasted for evening corn.

Every evening, while Bamaineo gathered wood, Echohawk took up his knife, scraped away the scales, then sliced open the fish. He pushed the entrails out with his thumbnail. Glickihigan started a fire while Echohawk threaded roasting sticks through the fish gills. While waiting for the fish to cook, they feasted on berries. At dusk they ate the roasted fish and drank cold water from the river.

Before sleeping, they cooled off with a swim. To ward off the mosquitoes, they slept under cedar branches. Echohawk fell asleep gazing at the stars, thousands of them, sparkling through the darkening canopy of trees.

In the afternoons Echohawk lay on his stomach, using his English clothes as a pillow. The hot sunshine loosened the muscles in his back and neck. The tension and terror he'd carried since Albany baked away along with his headache.

Anytime he was hot, all he had to do was scoop a handful of water out of the river and splash himself.

There was plenty of time to doze and think.

So much has happened since our mother died, he thought, reaching out to pluck a pawpaw from a drooping branch. *More than a year and a half since she began her next life.*

I remember how it was after her death. We stepped into her wigwam and stared in shock at the empty cooking pots and hollow bowls. Those pots and bowls were like our empty stomachs and our hollow hearts. Who would feed us? Take care of us? Tell us stories? Comb our hair? Mend our clothes and make us new ones?

We did all those things and more. We learned to cook and sew, we learned to take care of ourselves. We learned by doing. Our stomachs were full, but our hearts were still hollow.

Then came the deer hunt and my first trip to Saratoga-on-the-Hudson, *where we traded a great bearskin for Thunderpath. My Vision Quest came next, and, after that, school. I escaped from the Warners and found out about my first life. I was captured by the*

English and sent to Albany. *I escaped from Aunt Ruth only to be captured by the Iroquois. I escaped again.*

I have been shifting from one life to another and back again my whole life. But why? What is the Great Spirit trying to tell me?

Echohawk smiled when he thought about the little town of Saratoga-on-the-Hudson. It really hadn't been so bad. Mrs. Warner was kind and a good cook. He'd made friends there—Ian, John, and Loxpa.

The log cabins and the schoolhouse were made of wood, just like wigwams. As in the camp by the waterfall, all the dwellings were close to the river but not too close, in case of flooding. People in Saratoga-on-the-Hudson stored dried, salted foods for the winter, just as the Mohicans did.

He turned over onto his back. The sunshine warmed his chest, legs, and face. The air swelled with the fragrance of ripening berries and clean water. Immense stands of oak, maple, cherry, chestnut, hemlock, beech, and buckeye arched above him. When the river narrowed, the branches on the opposite banks touched and tangled together, like a green wigwam over his head. Squirrels chattered in the canopy of branches, crossing from riverbank to riverbank without getting their feet wet.

Echohawk felt the green within himself.

And I am not the only person who shifts from one life into another, Echohawk thought as he bit into his pawpaw. *Yellow Eel's son is learning to be a Delaware now that he is no longer Iroquois. Fawn and Smoke Eyes are learning to be English again, as Major Woodbridge did when he was captured from the Metoac. Red Fox must be making good* horseshoes *by now. Surely Celia and Sara are as English as my aunt Ruth.*

We all eat turkey, raccoon, squirrel, rabbits, and deer. We have taught the English to eat corn and squash; they have taught us to eat apples and doughnuts. *We have taught them to wear animal skins in winter; they have taught us to wear* cloth *in summer. We use their muskets; they use our bows and arrows.*

We both have harvest festivals at the Moon of Fallen Leaves and spring festivals at the Sugar Maple Moon.

So different yet so much alike. I remember telling Red Fox about the oak trees, how each one looks different and yet the trunks are the same.

Echohawk sat bolt upright. The raft tilted, sloshing water over his sleeping brother.

Bamaineo woke up sputtering. "What was that for?"

"We are all the same," Echohawk exclaimed.

"We are not," Bamaineo said crossly. "I am wet and you are dry." He scooped a handful of water up from the river and threw it at Echohawk. "There. Now we are the same."

"We are all the same," Echohawk repeated.

"What do you mean?" Glickihigan asked. He was sitting crosslegged at the back of the raft, using a flat piece of wood as a rudder.

"I have been shifting from one life to another since you found me in the log," Echohawk explained. "And I don't even remember my first life. Not really. I have one clear memory of a shaft of sunlight through a window made of *glass*.

"But the only way we can go from one life to another is if we are all the same. We find what is similar in that different life and cling to it," Echohawk said excitedly. "When you brought me from my first life to the camp by the waterfall, there must have been enough there, enough that was the same, for me to cling to."

"We are all the same," Glickihigan muttered uncertainly. He repeated it slowly, rolling the words in his mouth as though tasting something for the first time and trying to decide whether he liked it or not. "Yes, I suppose you are right."

Echohawk stretched out on the raft again. Bamaineo was making a game of cupping his hand on the river's surface and watching the water flow over it. The water looked as thick and heavy as maple syrup.

It was that brief moment in the Moon of Ripe Berries known as When Time Rests. The earth eases into perfect balance, and nothing changes except the rain and the sun's rising and setting.

The night air was as warm as the endless afternoons. The dawntime was as warm as the dusk.

The river water was becoming no warmer, but it was not yet becoming cooler. The leaves grew no greener or bigger, but they had not yet begun to change color. The birds were no longer taking care of their young, but they were not yet flying south. The animals were not yet foraging for winter food or looking for places to hibernate. The People were no longer planting, but it was not yet time to harvest.

It was as though nature herself, for one shining moment, stretched out her arms to their full width and height to revel in her own beauty, before shrinking back with the approaching cold and decay.

Bamaineo jumped up with a shout.

On the riverbank were men, almost as tall and slender as saplings.

Glickihigan raised his right hand and called out, "Mohican."

"Susquehannan," one of them called out.

"Where are you going?" another called out slowly. Their languages were similar.

"To the Three Sisters," Glickihigan called back, slower still.

"Our river breaks in two not far from here," another one shouted. "Follow her western half upstream until the very end, then portage west over the hill to the beginning of the Mahoning River. She will lead you into the Allegheny and then the Three Sisters."

"Yes," Bamaineo called back.

The tallest Susquehannan shouted, "There is a

camp south of here. You will reach it by evening corn. Ask for my clan and they will feed you." He opened his shirt to reveal his tattoos. "I am Turtle clan. Ask for the Turtle clan."

"We are Turtle clan too!" Bamaineo shouted. "We're the same!"

Echohawk said softly, "We are all the same."

AFTERWORD

ABOUT CAPTIVES

In the first chapter, Adam Watkins mentions
Eunice Williams. Her kidnapping by Canadian
Mohawks and her subsequent refusal to return to
Massachusetts was a well-known story throughout
New England in the first half of the eighteenth
century.

In late February 1704 five-year-old Eunice was
kidnapped from her home in Deerfield,
Massachusetts, and taken to a Mohawk town not
far from Montreal, Canada. Her father, John
Williams, was a well-known pastor, and when he
found her, he was determined to get her back. But
Eunice was already living with a Canadian Mohawk
family and didn't want to return. She married and

spent the rest of her long life (she died in 1785) as a French- and Mohawk-speaking Catholic.

Eunice Williams was one of hundreds of captives taken from frontier towns and outposts in the seventeenth and eighteenth centuries. Some were taken north to Canada. Others disappeared into the New England wilderness.

The colonial governments were in a quandary about captives. On the one hand, if they agreed to pay an official price for captives, that would only encourage more kidnappings. On the other hand, if they refused to pay any money, the captives' families would call their governments cruel and uncaring.

For those captives living in Canada the colonial governments had no choice but to give money quietly to the Captivity Society of New England. This charity would then give the money to the French colonial government, who in turn would pay the Mohawk, Ottawa, Abenaki, or Huron kidnappers. Often years would go by before the families were reunited.

Captives living in New England were sought out and returned individually. Often the army would find them in remote villages, or an unhappy captive would look for an opportunity to escape and turn himself in.

Quite often, and this was especially true with children, the captives didn't want to return. A child's life was hard in the New England settlements, with little time for games or play. Their time was spent in school, in church, or working on the farm. For these children, "becoming a savage" must have been like breaking out of a prison.

On October 21, 1743, the Massachusetts Common Court really did offer Eunice Williams and her Mohawk husband money if they would move permanently to Massachusetts. They refused.

The Captivity Society of New England sent former captives into churches to plead the cause of other captives. On those Sundays the money in the collection plates would be used to ransom those still held in captivity.

❖ ❖ ❖

In 1754 the British had a fort called Fort Pitt (now Pittsburgh, Pennsylvania) where the Allegheny and Monongahela Rivers merge to form the Ohio River.

Ten years later, in 1764, the English sent word to all their Indian neighbors in Ohio and Pennsylvania that any whites living among them had to be returned to Fort Pitt. The British made a treaty with the Delaware and other tribes in the area. As long as every white captive was returned, the British would not allow pioneer settlements in the Northwest Territory—what is now Ohio, Indiana, Illinois,

Michigan, and Wisconsin. Families were broken up, and whites who'd lived their whole lives as tribal members started new lives as British colonists.

The British kept their word. Except for a few missionaries, no whites were allowed farther west than Fort Pitt. After the Revolutionary War the British lost their thirteen colonies, and newly minted Americans flooded into the Northwest Territory.

ABOUT THE PATROONS

The Dutch patroons were a holdover from New Amsterdam, which became British New York in 1664. The Dutch West India Company gave a patroon either sixteen miles of land on one Hudson riverbank or eight miles of land on opposite riverbanks. The patroon needed to persuade fifty men and their families to live within the settlement for at least one year. He became their patroon, or patron.

Within their own domains the patroons controlled the hunting, fishing, and milling rights as well as the civil and criminal courts. They could appoint their own magistrates and were entitled to one tenth of the harvests.

The Dutch Crown promised ten tax-free years to each patroon settlement. The patroons were encouraged to buy African slaves from the Dutch slave ships. These ships would drop anchor first in

New Amsterdam, then sail up the Hudson to Albany. The New York State Legislature banned slavery in 1827.

After 1664 the directors of the British West India Company (not connected with the Dutch West India Company) persuaded the governors of the newly British colony of New York to allow the patroons to keep their power and influence along the banks of the upper Hudson. The Dutch had no standing armies in New York; British troops were assigned to the patroons to maintain order.

The Dutch stronghold of Fort Orange on the upper Hudson was a great trading center for northeastern North America. The British renamed the town Albany. Furs from the west, and finished goods from Europe and the European colonies, were bought and sold there. The patroons arranged for the Indian House to be built for Native American traders who came from as far away as Hudson Bay. Albany was also the clearinghouse for captives, who, along with furs, rifles, rum, and teapots, were brought there to be traded.

Albany's modern-day Broadway, or Route 32, was called Market Street in the eighteenth century.

ABOUT THE DELAWARE

After their lands filled with Europeans, the Delaware had no choice but to move west. The journey itself was dangerous because it meant traveling through Iroquois lands. Instead of heading west from Albany to Lake Otsego, then taking the Susquehanna River south, Glickihigan, Bamaineo, and Echohawk first had to walk south through the Catskills. Only then could they turn west and find a roundabout way to the Susquehanna.

These days there are only about two thousand people who can call themselves Delaware. They live in Oklahoma and in Ontario, Canada. The Stockbridge-Munsee band of Mohicans lives in Wisconsin.

ABOUT ECHOHAWK

Was Echohawk a real person? No, but he easily could have been. Historians think as many as thirty percent of eighteenth-century Native Americans living in the eastern woodlands were captives. Not all of them were white captives, of course. Since prehistoric times, tribes had been taking captives from other tribes to replace loved ones who had died.

Echohawk would have been twenty-nine years old in 1764. Would he have surrendered to Colonel Henry Bouquet and walked from the Tuscarawas River to Fort Pitt? There would have been nothing for him there. Surely he would have headed west instead of turning himself in.

SOURCES

Arden, Harvey. "The Iroquois: Keepers of the Fire." *National Geographic,* September 1987, pp. 370–403.

Demos, John. *The Unredeemed Captive: A Family Story from Early America.* New York: Alfred A. Knopf, 1994.

Hyde, George E. *Indians of the Woodlands: From Prehistoric Times to 1725.* Norman, Okla.: University of Oklahoma Press, 1962.

Kennedy, William. *Albany: Improbable City of Political Wizards, Fearless Ethnics, Spectacular Aristocrats, Splendid Nobodies, and Underrated Scoundrels.* New York: Viking Press, Washington Park Press, 1983.

King, Titus. *Narrative of Titus King of Northampton, Mass., a Prisoner of the Indians of Canada, 1755–1758.* Reprint: Hartford, Conn: Hartford Historical Society, 1938.

Saunders, Linda. Stillwater Historical Society, Stillwater, N.Y.

Savage, James. *A Genealogical Dictionary of the First Settlers of New England. Showing Three Generations of Those Who Came Before May, 1692, on the Basis of Farmer's Register.* Baltimore: Genealogical Publishing Co., 1990.

Van der Zee, Henri and Barbara. *A Sweet and Alien Land: The Story of Dutch New York.* New York: Viking Press, 1977.